Beautiful Moon

Wakes Me Up Before the Sunlight

A NOVEL

D1736307

Maria Alice Silva-Amey

outskirts
press

"...Lives of great men all remind us
We can make our lives sublime,
And, departing, leave behind us
Footprints on the sands of time."

A Psalm of Life -Henry Wadsworth Longfellow

One day Lara Alberene saw her dreams break apart, and saw her visions slow down and pause. It wounded Lara's heart; but she began following a new direction and looking for a new destination!

Here Lara was, trying to understand her heritage and avoid hearing members of her family always compare her behaviors with someone else in the family. Was this okay? Both good and bad had occurred in the cycle of family life. Lara had to figure things up and learn how to deal with all these judgmental comparisons in her life. When she began examining her own image she became the most curious person in the world. In the first part of this novel, Lara is looking for more information and direction regarding her great-great grandparents, and to know about her family's genetic behaviors .... She grew scared and always placed herself back into what she considers reality. "Someone in my family history did something bad..." "I'm a bad person, this will happen to me." "It will suffocate my children, and I'm going to die."

Lara seemed drawn by issues closer to the heart; she was always gasping for air, as she followed her dreams. These sweet dreams constantly uncovered memories that motivated her to continue her adventure.

Lara, in the second district, began to feel a very vivid pain, memories rose up about her offensive cousin, and her endless freedom from punishment. Lara lived in this mute world. Sometimes she would hear only the echo of a distant cry in her silence.

At the beginning of her career, her jobs were not reliable. It seemed earth was upside-down, and she had always been scared. Lara sometimes felt her body being drawn into the Blue Moon. Lara always was looking for figurative images in her search for love, but she could not seem to trust it. Life was complicated, full of drama and anxiety, offering only fading illusions. Her past was bringing a whole new contact with reality and a huge sense of the possibility of living a normal life.

1

What is the magic, the ritual, and the godsent message that calls, makes your wish, your awareness, your connections to your past? You must see yourself clearly, make a wish, let it connect with a romantic moment, or spiritual visions, and sometime if it is your lucky day, the Blue Moon may bring you an opportunity you cannot resist. That is the beginning. I've been exploring my internal thoughts, and the trajectory of my heritage. Some facts are clear to me and some are hidden behind me. At times I have no ideas and I must attempt to find them. I don't want to think too much, but a little more information would help me find the truth. I believed that my inheritable factors are hard-wired into my internal reflection, but I care less about the fact that I need to know my ancestors, and more about believing in facts and reality.

I began to make my own judgments regarding my heritage and avoid any contact with nagging doubts—comments that arise from the deep pit of uncertainty. Words, investigation, judgment, comparison, just like that or look alike and go on. All these facts make me wonder: should I be walking carrying keys to my future destiny that will keep me focused on my own reality and my internal luck? I will start with my name, Lara, named after my great-great-grandmother.

My father had the same feelings as I. He believed that once you are born everything good comes to you from GOD and from your own vision and experience. But whom are we following? Again, my father had his moments of imbalance; who escapes it entirely? Before he met my mother, he was a traveling man.

I borrowed his insight and began to adopt my way of doing things and I still think that chance can bring you luck. I noticed that as soon as I began creating ways to help me release my stress, most of the time I'd fall prey before I could stop. It was related to bad energy passing through my body.

I had to spend my last two years dealing with work environment, employing my ability to explain facts that were or were not in my power, and in my toolbox of experience. I was so used to being blamed for things that I couldn't even imagine. I began to realize that these could be inheritable factors that combined to make me become and act this way.

But there were certain obligations, that, I, Lara had to cover, and once I grew older, I was calling on each one to take their responsibility and name people who get involved in things that should not even be allowed. I was able to understand that some of my bizarre judgments would break apart a rock. So, I began standing up for my views and selecting and explaining my part in each project.

My parents always told me, "Lara, always make sure to do your best and give yourself the option of doing the right thing." My father would tell me of the lack of lionesses. He said most women do not have the courage to reflect clean moral power, and truly be there in the moment. Sometimes, I thought that it was better not to be there, so I did not need to do any deal or answer comments on decisions with which I had nothing to do, and I tried to keep most explorations to myself.

I don't recognize people that like to always say that facts happened because the fate was already set. In other words, humans cannot alter their own fates or the fates of others. I thought that it spread negativity if people could not change the future; and everything was the way that it was supposed to be.

So, I began to hear about my own family's story. And, growing up I also read so many weird stories from past generations; it made me wonder how it could all be real. So, I stopped for a minute and said: how did this happen and how did people manage with so many issues and differences? It seemed overwhelming to identify me as Lara, an individual who had her own manners or offered another way to dig deep into family cycles.

2

I have heard people ask me, where I'm from; they keep guessing: Indian, African Latina, White/Caucasian. I do not believe that matters. I didn't care. And I told them, "I am what your eyes see" and, also, I told them to "check and see what your heart feels."

I will be thirty-four next month. No one from my family ever asked me how growing up was with this crazy background or that sort of luck. Paying attention I wouldn't even try to understand because I fit perfectly into my family cycle. I guess in my family community, whether me and my sisters and brothers heard people saying we were irrational, I sealed myself in a blanket and asked my mother, "Do you see yourself as irrational sometimes?"

I remembered a day when I was traveling to Spain , this couple insisted on getting information speaking in Spanish.

I said, "Lady, I do not understand." They both got so mad, the man insulted me by saying loudly, "You don't want to speak your native language," and then he said the "Frick," word in Spanish.

I was scared and asked, "What did I say that was wrong?"

I still faced people confused with my heritage and I don't have to get into the conversation because it seems a hot button with them. When I first started working at the Lab occasionally someone asked me, "Did you get in here by completing courses or did someone inappropriately help you get in?"

And I asked them, "Tell me first how you got here as a manager of this big lab? I assumed that you also passed the test, right?"They became unhappy when I explained that the Lab was not my chosen place to work when I didn't understand the vision of the company. But I did want to follow their policies of sometimes using organs that are infected to do an experiment.

I ended up staying in the company for three years; and when I saw crooked activity, I left. They charged me with breaking some protocols that I alleged were not safe for human beings, and I could prove it.

I felt that I was ready for this position, but when I saw what they were doing with human tissue, I stopped working there. I had to sign my contract of resignation.

"I was coming to work very dissatisfied," I said to my father many times.

"Oh," he said. Then he remembered, it also happened with him.

I said, "I know. Again!"

The month I was at the Lab I could not sleep well. My nights were a nightmare, because I needed to report the Lab procedure., I felt I must break the protocol and explain that the Lab was still selling organs, plus was in the process of duplicating many different organs such as kidneys, heart and everything else they could duplicate and sell: legs, arms, hair... One coworker said, "I'm leaving too. I hear that a twelve-year-old girl was poised to sell five feet of her hair." And I asked her, "Is the requisition from this Lab?"

She said, "I don't know, I'm not sure if it is."

I felt sick, my stomach quickly began to ache, and I went outside for some fresh air.

I kindly asked my coworker, "What do you think you want to do?"

She said, "Oh, it's time for break," and quickly I understood that we shouldn't talk about these issues at the Lab because it was our workplace. So, we took a few-minute break, and she said, "We need to report the way the Lab makes illegal transactions. It is organ trafficking, very similar to trafficking with live humans. The two of us did our part, told our versions of how the Lab was running. The Lab was under investigation and finally was closed.

Be a free young woman, I was told, I didn't very often and was not happy with the result at all. But, looking at my past, I recognized that I still faced telling the truth about Mariana. I understood the case was closed, but the truth was not set free; someone needed to know. I felt like a broken vase that was glued and painted, and everything appears beautiful only on the outside.

It took me a long time afterward to find a job. I suppose that my family understood and gave me the support I needed. For me their support was welcome at the moment. I had a degree in molecular biology, and no work experience regarding business- -only when I worked at a young age helping my father with his store. But my job was wrapping stuff and putting it in the bags. I was invited on a job interview with another Bio Lab; the round table interviewers liked my answers and a couple weeks after my interview they called me. I loved the job and the work environment though I heard a lot of employees talked behind my back—maybe because they sensed that I was given someone else's position. I saw this approaching and made a poor judgment call about the job--that I could do better than them. At the beginning there was a sense of tension with some colleagues. But after being able to make friends and relax I began speaking and hearing people talk about vocation, parties and more things that I found out later--things that I never should know.

I heard family tell stories about when Brazil conducted its first official census, the population was 9,930,478 in 1872 and my great great grandparents were part of this census. It was just 16 years before slavery's official abolition in 1888. Modern estimates place Brazil's total population in 1872 at approximately 10.3 million; the exclusion of non-white infants and indigenous populations from the census is likely the cause of this deficit.

My great-uncle was a fine upstanding slave. Two years after I met him, my great-uncle was beaten to death for disrespecting his master in Maceo. It is often the case that, when a human is mistreated by other humans, the claim is made that the victim was treated "like an animal." What is meant by this expression is that the victim has not been treated with any recognition of their moral value.

Years passed and many people died of hunger

because of the great drought that happened at the time. Most of my relatives did not survive. I remember my family said that they were craving for food—for anything that could offer some good nutrients. As I grew up, I heard my grandfather saying that they eat ants as a form of nutrition to replace protein as an uneasy sensation occasioned by the lack of food. My mother always said, "We had a small meal; it wasn't enough to satisfy my hunger." Many people's weakened condition was worsened by the prolonged lack of food.

Many people moved, including some of my past relatives. They moved to Mossoro, which later was the first city in Brazil to abolish slavery, and at thirty years of age, my great-great grandfather was free.

At this time my great-great grandparents were eight years old, but I already heard the comments that a law "the Lei Aurea" abolished the remains of slavery. My great great-grandfather met my great great-grandmother during the second revolt of the Armanda where she worked as a nurse born in France. Here the conflict started?

My grandfather would say, "If I liked to write, I would have written one of the greatest novels ever read in Brazil."

At just eight years of age my great-great grandfather, did not know the alphabet, so he couldn't read or write, and it took many years for him to be able to read. At the time census data was not available. A common method used to estimate literacy was to calculate the number of people who could sign official documents such as paper court documents, marriage certificates, or a simple signing of your name.

As soon as my great grandfather turned eighteen, he said: "I am going to the military."[1] At the time he was working at Ford selling cars, and the following year, 1905, he went to serve a military year. In another part of the Americas, United States faced the shooting of protesting factory workers in St. Petersburg, sparking what became known as the 1905 Revolution, the 20th century's first major challenge of the country. That event affected the Brazilian workers. On the South side, we had Joaquim Nabucco appointed first Ambassador to the United States.

There was much conversation surrounding the family table, and the community at the time. The following year my uncles were part of the First Brazilian Workers' Congress. It also was the year that my great grandmother met my great grandfather. At that time, you could hear anywhere that the people only spoke about the storytelling of my great great-grandparents. So, the storytelling continue so I understood my great grandparents.

For love, my great-grandfather would have killed himself in a hiding place already 600,000 kilometers away from the farm where he lived, wrote several letters before he died and, in the letters, said: "I died because I knew that all of you from Batur Ipe do not accept my marriage with my great-grandmother because she was a white lady. My great-grandfather was a black man, and there were more stories. Mr. Colonel wanted to sell my great grandfather in order to stop the marriage, and sent great-grandmother away, just because she was in love with a black men.

My great grandfather set up a historical account that was available to the family and to the rest of the community. Many people outside would have access to the family story. It was clear that the plot would change their lives forever. The historical data linked with that love can kill no longer. It can now be explained.

My great great-grandfather had a friend that he trusted; this person made him believe that death was the one way to prove his true love for my great great-grandmother. But why was this person allowed to kill my great grandmother if Mr. Colonel simply wanted to make their lives miserable?

It seemed that the abolished did not overcome. And my great grandfather said, "If someone tries to force this person to say something, they may regret it, and so we will settle scores up there."

My great great-grandmother did know who was taking care of her for me. Maybe when she knew I would have a day anywhere in heaven?" he said, "or in hell did they settle wounds with her, or ask for a thousand pardons?"

When this letter arrived in the hands of colonel Machado, the coronel was mad. From the moment the search began, the city learned of the love that the coronel's daughter had in relationship with the black men at the house, the comments were so common that anywhere and at any time one only heard of the shame that the coronel's daughter had pressed upon the family, for others the conversation was one of regret, for others it was a proof of true love.

3

She was a rich, white girl–a nurse--who next year would go to Lisbon to attend medical school. She would be the first nurse in the city to study medicine in the countryside. At only twenty-three years of age, she graduated.

The next day the family received another envelope. When the colonel opened it, he found ashes and in the letter it said: "My parents do not think that it is someone else's, the ashes are from my body, the letter and the writing is also mine. Before I died, I wrote these letters and asked for the ashes to be delivered along with the letters."

She said, "Whoever put the ashes in this envelope is someone very special. I asked him to do it for me. Perhaps they do not believe that they can be mine for Mr. Coronel. "My great grandmother, would not be brave enough to do so." That was the way my great-grandmother would talk to my great great-grandfather.... "Brave as you are, my father, with your lies and power, you do things without thinking, without love."

I did it out of love. I had died otherwise, but it wouldn't do any good. You wouldn't know me. Mr. Colonel never bothered to meet my love. Death for Mr. Coronel doesn't matter, as do people.

"No need to send your crew to look for me; tomorrow you will receive another letter. Before I die, I left several letters. One you will receive any moment and the next will be written at the place where you can find the rest of the ashes."

The rumors run in that city. People did not believe how the romance of the Colonel's daughter, my great grandmother was so secretive for a long time. According to priest Abílio, he already knew. Since they were teenagers, the priest exhausted himself seeing the two playing in the stream.

Priest Abílio was now officially aware of the romance. He was the most respectful Priest of the community, and he focused on helping everyone who called and wanted to talk and asked for help, no matter what the situation.

Priest Abílio developed a successful church for all kinds of drama that a family can't resolve with different issues and challenges. These encompassed the situation of my great-great relatives – Priest Abílio worried and tried over and over to end the relationship. My great-grandparents always played together most of the day every day. It left priest Abílio wondering if this is not God's good will. My great grandfather felt passionate in a way he never had before. The connection seemed to be mutual; the more they stayed together, the more the love was growing. My great grandfather reached out to priest Abílio after he returned from Sao Paulo. He'd stayed away from the farm for a couple months. Since he'd been out of the community, my great grandmother told her parents about her love for my great-grandfather.

The Colonel had tried to distance both, but didn't understand that they wanted my great-grandfather to be some distance from the farm. But now my great grandparents were in love. They wanted to live a new life and priest Abílio tried to mediate.

My great grandparents were angry with the situation and the lack of comprehension. Colonel said, "When my great grandfather arrives at the farm, I will kill him." The colonel told this to all the workers and he gave order to shoot; my great mother would have no chance to see my great-grandfather, since he arrived from Sao Paulo. She'd hoped to see him for a little bit, at least to say that she loved him and wanted to run away. But my great mother tried to protect my great father feelings, and she wanted to wait for a chance as soon as her father went away for his next trip.

My great grandmother looked at her mother, who was just disappointed with her. "It's true? It is true you love [him]?"

My great grandmother didn't respond. And her mother yelled behind her. "You won't respond to me?" And she said, "I did everything for you and you can't even talk to me,"

My great-grandmother said. "Do you have any idea what it means to love someone?"

I cannot be closer to the person," My great grandmother said. Her mother paused, and my great grandmother had never seen her mother frizzy and quiet like that before.

My great-grandparents had entered the church in hiding and made communion with priest Abílio. My great grandparents tell me that it was not easy for the two teenagers to enter the church without people being able to see them, because at that time racism was violent, never a white man or white girl could walk with blacks in the streets. Imagine the Colonel's daughter entering the church with the daughter of the right profile men in the city.

My great grandfather was not as black as the other black men; he had his mother's eyes. She was a beautiful Indian woman, strong teeth, perfect, she was sold for less than five dollars to the Spanish Colonel. My great great-grandmother worked at the Colonel's house. The colonel wanted to sell my great great-grandmother, but the colonel's wife advised that it would be better for her to stay, and sell another. The wife said to colonel Frances, "She's the best slave we have. She has asked us not to sell her, for we will not create a quarrel because of this black." My great great- grandmother, had a daughter named Joana.

Joana remained on the farm and began dating Rubio. At the age of sixteen she became pregnant. Rubio was happy, and he decided to get married. He built a small house near the colonel's house, as Rubio had always been the colonel's right-hand man, and the colonel was always in need of the black. Now it should be known that the colonel had no patience to wait for things; he hardly called Rubio before the man was already at the door.

Months passed and Joana arrived at the beginning of the nine months, when the coronel's wife called her desperately to go and call Rubio in the sugarcane field. Running, there went Joana hardly being able to walk, to call her husband to the mistress.

There he hurried to Joana to call her husband. Rubio hurried to fetch the whole family, and the blacks were curious to know things. In a few hours the doctor left Amelia's room somewhat worried about what he knew, but finally said, to those in the room that were worried, "It was nothing serious, in a few months the Blue Moon farm will have a new heir."

4
_____

The astonishment on the faces of all the blacks was remarkable. With this, Rubio gave orders for everyone to go to work. The black Rubio had all the support to punish or give any order in the absence of the Colonel. At night Rubio and Joana talked about the pregnancy of Dona Amelia, who in the accounts was stated to already be almost three months old in the womb.

Ah, Joana, this fiasco is not going to be good news for the colonel," they murmured. When does he arrive?"

"Ten days from now, he will go to Portugal and then to Paris to do some negotiations, and travel a total of forty days off the farm."

Amelia did not have such a smooth pregnancy as did Joana. One day out of pure jealousy the madame threw several dishes on the floor with food and made

Joana clean it up--just wanting to see if Joana was still strong. If Rubio had been closer, this would not have happened. Rubio seemed to be brave, but if he could, he would give a party every night to the blacks of all the farms. Every day was impossible, but when a small party was celebrated it was reason for Rubio to celebrate the arrival of his son, because he was sure that it would be a boy and his son would be called Rubens Xavier. He would be so strong and intelligent that he would invent a device called an engine. He would be rich and respected and would also be free to travel all over of the world. The helpers were paying attention to Rubio's beautiful words.

Rubio on this day went to the city to talk to the colonel, owner of the Blue Moon farm, The colonel wanted to sell the farm, he was the one who sold Joana for cents on the dollar. And now he wanted to sell the farm, he lost everything. He sold the blacks and the farm was lonely. The old colonel wanted to go far away, but for that he needed to sell more things and only the farm remained, Rubio confirmed that the colonel wanted to buy the farm but would only bring the money on Monday, when he arrived from Paris with the rest of it – The servant, Rubio, told his owner that, he would wait until Monday at six in the afternoon, and no later. "Be on time, no minutes after.

Rubio returned as soon as possible; he had been out all day and did not leave his conviction that the son the great Rubens, would be born. When Rubio arrived, it was already getting dark and Joana was very ill. Rubio was in a hurry to call the midwife who started the port. Rubio's distress left everyone quiet. The midwife was nervous, the black women she was helping were amazed; the midwife had never been so nervous. She didn't know what to do. She asked, "Rubio, go and call the doctor" (and the only doctor he had was the doctor of the colonels' relatives). But Rubio had no choice but to go and ask the doctor to go to the farm.

It was useless for Rubio to go to the doctor's house. The doctor said, "I don't put my hand on servants." Rubio begged, almost kissed his feet, cried, but the doctor didn't go. Meanwhile the midwife asked Joana to help and be very calm because if her prayers did not fail, Joana was pregnant with two babies in her belly. The black women looked at each other and the face of astonishment was too much. Never had a woman given birth to two children in a single pregnancy on the farm. Joana was the first. At the same moment Dona Amelia burst into the room. She'd heard the midwife's intuitions, and in light of the situation she was a little worried, but soon left the room caressing her own belly.

5

In the room Joana tried to control herself for her, and for her two babies, that should be born soon, and with a lot of prayer revolving for Joana's safety, and the servant women around, and the experience of the midwife and many prayers in the room *it happened, the miracle,* the babies were apparently making their way down the birth canal. The black women continued to pray and the tears flowed without disturbing the prayers. On the ground the candles lit up as if it were the sky with the full Blue Moon and with many stars. Suddenly the prayers were broken by the lusty cry of a baby, the midwife had saved a baby, but now she was absolutely sure that the other baby was still in the belly. At this moment Rubio, saw the euphoria of everyone around his house, and the negroes cried, "Rubio, your son, Ruben, was born."

In the window Dona Amelia observed the joy of all,

but Rubio, when he was entering, was not so happy. Not because she was a girl but because the midwife said that Joana was without the strength to be able to take the other baby. She could not do anything else; Rubio came close to the bed, hugged Joana and said: "Joana, please find your strength and ask God to enlighten this child who is there inside you to shine out."

Joana replied simply, "I have no more strength," and fainted.

The midwife said *if* to my great grandfather, if he wanted to save his wife and his son, and in a great hurry, he had to take her to the nearest hospital. However to go to the hospital was impossible, it was too far. Or he had to convince Dona Amelia to seek out the doctor, if it took too long the child may die. Dona Amelia continued to observe the blacks celebrating, when Rubio left the room in silence, but very sad and leaving the blacks hanging down, as one by one they began to kneel. Dona Amelia, without understanding anything, sought to know what was happening, learned and sent for Rubio saying, "Prepare the fast carriage and we go get Doctor Mário." The eyes of Rubio saw two lamps, the pair followed silently and Dona Amelia prayed, as well as Rubio. When they arrived at the house of the doctor he was not there; he had gone to the farm. They were both waiting, Rubio outside and Dona Amelia in the room of the doctor's house. It did not take long for the doctor to arrive as he saw the black man in front of his house. And he was soon saying, "I'm not going to leave the house for anything–even if it were for the colonel, even less for your servant."

The midwife of the region was paid to take care of the pregnant women, not being your black woman who will make me leave here, and opened the door without letting Rubion explain and close the door, by the suppressed Dona Amelia who was waiting for him. They talked a few minutes in the office and the doctor said "to one of his maids." I will go to the Blue Moon farm, and I will return soon. Already knowing the case he took his helper to nurse and his briefcase with the preparations. I heard the orders of Dona Amelia but that was another story. They had secrets and never denied favor to each other.

I wondered what it would be? And Rubio was waiting anxiously until he saw Dona Amelia and Doctor Fernandes. Then a broad grin creased his cheeks. Thirty kilometers and they reached the farm. The house of Rubio had made a chain of many prayers and faith, all holding hands and in the center the image of Saints and many candles. Joana lay motionless. Dead or alive?

Only God knew. The doctor entered the room, and asked, "Everyone go outside." He only needed his helper and Joana." The midwife, insisted on staying to be able to see how the baby would be delivered. She had never seen a Cesarean section, and that was what the doctor planned to do.

The Cesarian was done very late and to the surprise of the doctor, Joana gave birth to another child who would be a boy, while Dona Amelia went to fetch the doctor. It was to finish killing Joana and what the population disbelieved in the beliefs of the midwives, the going of the doctor, it was to accuse the rotten midwife that she did this.

Dona Amelia was not satisfied that the black woman had fathered two children. The Doctor did a the Cesarean section, asked the nurse to stitch it and to bury the baby boy. The emotional state of Rubio was very grief-stricken. The doctor acted as if he saw zero sadness in the eyes Rubio, the consolations that the servants gave were: "Don't stay like this, Rubio, you have a daughter, and Joana will be fruitful and will bear several more children.

But before leaving the farm, the doctor said to Dona Amelia, "The servant, the black woman has no more life," and he said, "to tell you the truth, I think she died before the baby."

6

Rubio on the same night made a point of burying his son, little Rubens. Rubio crafted the coffin very tiny and when it was completed the pinewood was damp from Rubio's tears... The saddest time for Rubio was when he finished because then it truly punched him so hard; he looked like he might melt away like bitter chocolate.

In the community, everyone clutched candles in hand. The night was dark, the moon decided not to appear, and the stars did not have the strength to remain shining. The sadness not only stirred the blacks but all eyes turned skyward to streaks of lightning. The only way they knew to show their suffering was to weep and wail, their faces anguished for the mother and child. When they returned from the burial, it began to rain, and everyone repeated that the rains were like tears from heaven, to show the sadness God felt for the deaths of Rubio's son and Joana.

At dawn, before going to the sugarcane field, Rubio looked at Joana who seemed still asleep. Rubio looked for the second time and saw that it was an imagination, a strong thought of Rubio. The time of the event was recent, and it would be better if Joana could rest some more. When Joana fainted, it was exactly two o'clock in the morning. At three in the morning they buried Little Rubens. Rubio was thoughtful until five in the morning and went to the sugarcane field, like all the other blacks too. Things had to be in order. Tomorrow the Colonel would arrive with good and bad news. Rubio worked quietly and made sure to stay away from the mill, which lacked the engine that would be have been made by his son, Rubens.

It was time for lunch which was served in the shed near the large mill. Rubio asked one of the servants if Joana had woken up, and if she had eaten anything. The servant said no, that she had just walked up to the bedroom door and Joana was still asleep. Rubio began to get worried and went to the house, screamed for Joana, but the answer was only silence.

It was already 11 o'clock and Joana was still motionless. Rubio murmured, "Ah, my God this is not right, Joana is cold, weird, lifeless. Without the order of Dona Amelia, Rubio went to look for the doctor, lost his head, and was beaten by the doctor's henchman. The sun was already setting when Rubio returned to the farm, Joana was being veiled and at dusk would be buried next to little Rubens, the ruffle he wanted so much. With the accompaniment of many candles and prayers. Rubio would not have imagined that all this was purposeful. The sadness of Ruben would not fit in the existing space. But he could not forget that Joana had left a daughter who had no name yet. It had been two days and Rubio had not seen his daughter. When he saw her my great grandfather was enthusiastic about the beauty of this girl who in the instant named her Helen.

The colonel Machado arrived a day late, the ship had some problems. Apparently for the colonel everything was in order. The only question he asked Rubio was "Black, this states you agreed to purchase the Blue Moon farm?"

"Yes, Mr. Colonel."

"Leave the carriage ready and we will soon talk to the colonel." The night passed quickly, and at dawn they went out with a few more goons arriving at the farm. The colonel was having coffee at that huge table by himself. The two colonels entered the office and stayed more than an hour. At the door they were on guard for Rubio and the henchmen when three well-dressed men arrived. One was a lawyer, then there was the judge and the clerk to pass the farm to colonel Machado. They stayed more than two hours in that room. When the Colonel left with the deed in his name, he did not believe that he owned the bloody farm. Tomorrow even colonel Marques would leave the farm. With the money he bought a small ship and put the de Ville de Boulogne II on the high seas, where he spent his last days. He did everything so that there was a shipwreck. Thus his death was identical to the sinking of the great ship "Ville de Boulogne I" where his sons died, his wife, and his parents. So was the end also of the colonel on the high seas destined for Paris. But I am jumping far ahead in my story. You do wish to know it all---every detail, am I right?

The colonel returned to the farm very satisfied, and I began to ask several questions, wanting to know the news of the region. Rubio replied: "Mr. Colonel, if there was any news in the region, I possess not a pennyworth of interest."

"But as a black Ruby?"

Rubio lowered his head, and said:

"Joana and my son Rubens, buried three days ago, though she did give me a beautiful daughter."

Startled, the colonel asked:

"Joana had children in her belly?"

"Yes, colonel, she was expecting two babies. And soon you will have your heir as well."

The Colonel made himself appear happy and anxious to get to the farm. At the lunch time, Dona Amelia informed the colonel of her pregnancy. Once again the Colonel was very proud, and at the lunch was present priest Abílio and the Machado family. He left the table feeling betrayed, he knew that this son was not his. He had gone to France only to do some tests and heal, but no one knew, he did not have the courage to say that he could not have children, yet suddenly his wife was pregnant. He could never survive hearing from the people that the powerful and respectable colonel Machado was the husband of a woman who practiced adultery. It would be a scandal permeating society in the region of Ceara. The colonel was not home enough to make a son. This would be one of the comments that society would make, and the shame would kill him.

In the afternoon the colonel left to go to the city, it was raining but he would make it in time. The roads were not yet asphalted, and it seemed that rain did not help too much. The colonel would roam far from the farm. He insisted on driving, but his car got stuck in the mud. He disembarked and tried to move, but it was raining so heavily he could only move the car about thirty yards ahead. Instead, still angry and brokenhearted the Colonel unfastened one of his horses and took a long ride, until the sun went down.

Dona Amelia was worried, gazing through the front doorway wearing a raincoat and her rain boots, she looked around for her husband. She had a feeling that something was not right. After dinner she would ask …. Usually, colonel didn't share much about things with her. And Dona Amelia assumed his behavior would be related to some of his business decisions. She walked around for some minutes, then back to the house. Hours later, colonel was home, very wet. His expensive boots were completely covered with mud.

Dona Amelia asked, "What is wrong?"

Colonel, couldn't even speak, and went straight to the bathroom for a shower and change of clothes

"I was worried about you," Amelia said.

"No worries," he said.

"Why you got so wet?" Dona Amelia asked.

Without looking at her, he said, "I was at the ban and one part of the ban is not covered." Colonel wanted to ask the simple question that was killing him, but he didn't want to tell her that he had a big health problem. This was how he saw not being able to have children. It was a generational problem. Again, he knew that because his great father was neglectful. The kids were born with birth defects and no doctor's care. Every time this happened, no medicines were provided for these kids. So, colonel had to pay for the failures of that family cycle.

The storm was still ferocious and Dona Amelia went to bed without colonel. That was not a big concern because she was used to sleeping by herself with the colonel gone for weeks, or some nights he stayed at his office for hours. He responded that he needed to work on some errands.

7

In the morning, the sky was clear and everything sparkled. And, colonel Machado decided to keep quiet and be happy with the arrival of his son. After a few months Dona Amelia was already in the seventh month of pregnancy when the colonel asked, "Will it be a girl or a boy?" But he waited for no answer and left quickly. Passing by Joana's house, he stopped and entered the room where Helen was. The Colonel stared at her for a long time. When a black woman came in the Colonel disguised his voice and said: "Colonel is looking for Rubio," and left.

At the end of the eighth month, the doctor would more often see the patient's condition, and the colonel would discreetly observe the doctor's countenance.

The days went by and on May 19, 1943 at 6:00 pm, at the Blue Moon farm was born, Fabricio.

The colonel sat indignant noticing that the child did not look like him, but the shame made him remain silent. However the comments in the region were that the colonel's son looked like him and that the boy was beautiful. To the colonel the boy had the face of the family doctor. And Dona Amelia knew that the son was his.

Months and years passed and Fabricio and Helen were five years old. The two ran away to play, because they already knew that the children of colonels and the children of slaves could not stay together. But for the two children this ruling did not exist.

When Helen, turned ten years old, Fabricio invited her to go to the creek, that he would be there waiting for her because he wanted to give her a gift. Helen arrived at the creek but did not see Fabricio. Knowing he was often oblivious, she waited for him. While she waited, in the distance the colonel Machado spotted her and came closer to observe her. He felt something strange, but he remained hidden and silent. It didn't take long before the two children started talking, playing and running. Fabricio said, "Helen, if you catch me, I'll give you a present. Helen dashed behind Fabricio, grabbed him and the two fell on the grass, curled up and laughed uproariously--the pair seemed created for each other."

The colonel Machado kept spying, but did not hear what they said. Suddenly Fabricio took something out of his pocket and gave it to Helen. It was a beautiful ring that Fabricio had bought in the city--of course, it was hidden.

The colonel Machado kept thinking, to society it was he and his son, and the colonel's son did not associate with children of slaves. He could not let these meetings happen anymore. He resolved to arrive furious and frightening to the children, being very severe and chastising Helen. His plan failed miserably.

And next year Fabricio would no longer have teachers at home; he would have to stay all week in the city to study. Fabricio began to revolt against his father. But all weekend he went to the farm, and always stayed with Helen, becoming expert at hiding, Thus, the years went by and more difficulties and obstacles would arise for Fabricio, and the longing that Fabricio felt was enormous for Helen. The colonel sent him to study even further, and the distance was a strong obstacle for Fabricio to stay without visiting the farm. And the hatred and frustration were growing more and more between Fabricio and the his father.

Helen was twenty years old, and still continued on the farm as a slave, despite having a lighter color. The colonel made her a slave to show society. The age difference between Helen and Fabricio was only four months. Fabricio the beautiful young man, educated, finished his studies to go to Lisbon and attend law school. It was a method that the colonel arranged to send his son far away; and it was also usual for rich children to go to Portugal to learn such fields as law or medicine.

8

The young Fabricio decided to change history, decided to assume the true love he felt for Helen. Then my great grandfather, Rubio, sought him in the city and confessed the truth about Helen and who really was his father. When I met Joana, she was expecting Helen. The colonel was very fond of going to his room; I heard Joana ask several times for the love of God, not to do anything with her, even though I was already with Joana, he forced me to stay with him. If she did not stay, he promised to do absurd things. Once, coming back early from the sugarcane field, I heard an argument – Joana said, "I'm pregnant..."

The colonel Machado laughed and said, "This child is not mine, and you're black. And another problem, I cannot have children."

Joana insisted, and she was threatened. The

colonel said, marry the servant, Rubio, he likes you. Marry replied, "I also like Rubio very much, I have to tell the truth."

The colonel replied, "If you count, you shall see I will kill the three and more. I will buy your grandparents and have them killed too, as well as the daughter.

Joana had remained silent about this heartache and ended up dying for us. And more Fabricio, I do not want to pit you against your family, but it was your mother who caused the death of Joana. "Your mother knew or wondered whether Joana was pregnant by the colonel, but never said anything and this grave secret caused Joana to suffer until she died."

Fabricio listened quietly.

Rubio asked Fabricio to look into his eyes. He needed to make sure he could trust him. Fabricio looked and said – "You can speak, my friend."

"Fabricio, what I want to tell you is that I love Helen as if she were my true daughter, and I know that you love her too. It's been two months since your mother has become very sick; maybe she will go soon, sorry to say so.

I saw the colonel approaching Helen a few months ago, sir. Fabricio noted that the colonel began to take an interest in Helen. To Rubio the colonel was approaching Helen to do what he did to Joana, but in fact he was not. He had received some correspondence, and the letter said that he could always have a child. He went on to be sure that Helen was his daughter and approached all to tell the truth; but she never had the courage and for Rubio things were reversed. But this approach between Helen and the colonel could not exist. The colonel did not know one hundred percent that Helen was his daughter, but I knew. I approached Fabricio, and said, "You can help me. Do you love Helen?"

He said, "More than anything in my life."

"But there's one more problem, Fabricio, that must be resolved, for the colonel claims you're not his son."

Fabricio became pale and startled.

As I told you, "He told Joana that he couldn't have children and suddenly Dona Amelia got pregnant with you."

"How can you claim that Helen is not your daughter?"

"That's sure, my young man, but I swore to myself that I wouldn't do anything, because you know what the colonel could have done, but even I never stopped loving Joana.

The Colonel thinks that he cannot have children, I believe, that for him you are a torment, that he loves sending you to study abroad, far away, to get rid of you."

"But if he's so sure it's not my father, why didn't he do anything?"

"Perhaps he was ashamed of the comments that society might make."

"That's why he hates me so much, but for him to be suspicious, is there anyone else who can be my father? Do you know or have you any idea who would have an affair with my father, Rubio?"

"I'm not sure, but he thinks it's the family doctor for all of you including the registration of his son. The only person who knew he couldn't have children was Mary, [colonel Machado old friend] nor does Amelia know. But as you now know, he was wrong. Now it remains to be seen whether you are really his son or not."

9

On the farm the colonel became a restless man who could not sleep, spent long nights on the porch, and when the night closed in with no remnants of daylight, the old colonel was alone thus ending his miserable nights and days. In the morning the colonel would have his coffee and go to the Blue Moon farm,. However, after he began receiving the mail from abroad, his suspicions could no longer be doubted, and he began to go crazy. He did not know now whether or not Fabricio could be his son. As for Helen being his daughter, there was also a possibility, but how could he resolve it? There must be a way to know the truth, but how?

Should he make Dona Amelia confess if she cheated with the doctor? Should he grill Rubio with raving questions as to whether he is sure that Helen is his daughter?

I couldn't get past this point of high despair. In Marjara, a small town in Cearra, not far from the Blue Moon farm, there would be a sample of a model of an engine for someone with ingenuity, where he gathered the big farmers and merchants. At the end of the meeting, the colonel received an invitation to lunch at the house of Mister Novato. Mister Novato was one of the largest merchants of Marjara, and some more farmers were invited, in order to talk more about the new economies that they could have if they acquired the new model of ingenuity. They had stars in their eyes regarding the economy of the country, of politics and projects for the new industrialization of the future. Then in 1923 the new innovation, the first radio broadcasting station, Radio Society of Rio de Janeiro.

When they talked about the future, it was a reason for them to talk about their children – because they took pride in the future and their offspring, "Do you know about the new novelty in the city? asked Mr. Naruto. "In Ceara we have the best doctor and even though he is the best, he cannot do anything for himself."

The very curious Colonel asked, "What is it? Do you know?"

"Well, his wife and mine are both very close friends, and the doctor has been undergoing treatment for almost thirty years and could not get her pregnant. In the next month they will go to Rio de Janeiro to adopt a child.

The reaction of the powerful farmers was astonishing. At dawn on October 1929, when the US stock market crashed, the Colonel received a letter from Fabricio. In the letter he read, "I have written this letter, and a few more that I will receive yet, before I die. Now reading this letter you can be sure that you will never see me anywhere on this planet again. And at this moment also the people are already aware of my true love for Helen. At this moment if everything went well, as I had asked before I died, millions of leaflets will be scattered throughout the region, and people will discover, by reading and learning how and what is a true love. It's no use, Colonel; you won't be able to gather all the leaflets.

And really the whole city was already learning that the Colonel's son and the slave Helen hid a twenty-year romance, for the two of them love was born when they both came into the world. And every week the Colonel would get a letter and never find out who left them on the farm.

Two years passed, and many things changed. Dona Amelia passed away and it was Helen who was taking care of the house. Rubio was tired, old, and not understanding of the changes in that house. In the evening Rubio would have to meet with Fabricio. In these two years of Fabricio's disappearance, the Colonel became very ill. Before Dona Amelia died, she confessed that she had never attracted him, and that she knew the Colonel realized Fabricio was not his son, but he never asked. "What he knew how to do was ignore me and mistreat Fabricio. For the Colonel to ask for forgiveness it seemed too late.

One night Rubio headed to the city, without realizing that someone was following him. Rubio entered Fabricio's hideout. At dawn on that farm, the people were agitated, the Colonel sent for the lawyer, the clerk, and priest Abílio feeling that he was on the verge of death and wanting to confess before the priest sent Rubio into the Colonel's room.

The priest said to Rubio, "Forgive him, the end of the Colonel has come."

"Forgive me, Rubio, the deep silence kills, I confess my end has come." - Ruben meant something but it was a veiled comment.

"The Colonel handed him a letter and said, he delivered this letter to my son, Fabricio." –

Rubio was frightened. He said, "I met my son through the letters. I had the chance to live next to Helen, but I was a coward, please Rubio, deliver this letter to her too."

"Don't look at me like that; you had both of them as children always by your side. Helen loves you, told me that you are the best father, and Fabricio knew you as a father, as a friend, in a great home, Rubio- I ask you to continue taking care of both of them, as you always did."

Coronel... "Don't say anything rubberish, just forgive me. At the funeral, said José Carlos, my great grandfather, who had so many people, that only afterward they noticed that it was because of the presence of Fabricio. The next day he felt sad and more than a little sorry about everything, and had not lessened the doubt regarding whether or not he was really the colonel's son but whom could he ask now?

10

To tell the truth, Fabricio was afraid to know who his father really was, for he loved Helen so much, and nothing would separate them. Suddenly a painful memory came to mind. Seventeen years ago in that same place the memories were cut off by the presence of Rubio. –

Fabricio, was your search fruitful, today was when Helen told me she could meet you here.

"So, tell me, what does my friend Rubio want?"

"The Colonel asked me to deliver this letter to you..."But like Rubio, he knew I was dead."

"I don't know how he found out, my young man."

"Fabricio, maybe the letter can answer your question." "I will retire so that I can read your letter in peace. Oh! My young man, your father asked me to deliver a letter to Helen, and she asks you to read it to her later.

"Sure," he said, "tell her 'Yes'."

Fabricio very tremulously opened the letter , and in silence read each line very carefully, sometimes stopping to wipe away the tears that blurred his vision. At the end of the letter, it said: "I didn't know how to love you, I didn't want to know you for thinking; I don't even want to remember. A father's advice, even if I was not a right father, look for the reasons before acting, look for the truth before judging, – forgive me for not acting like a man, like a father, but I learned to love you since I learned that you were my son, but at the same time I went crazy, knowing that I had lost you.

One of these nights, very sick and tired, I decided to go behind Rubio's when I found out that you were not dead. I swear, I could not get in. If you entered, I would have died at that moment, and things would be half over--this letter would not be penned. I know the script is tremulous, but I managed to write everything I wanted. Look for the family lawyer, your name is in the will, you and my son."

Fabricio finished reading the letter, sighed and took courage to speak to Helen upon finding her in her room. My grandmother was crying desperately, which not even Fabricio could control. The Colonel would never be her father.

Fabricio, asked for the letter to read, and it was

handed to him. In the letter it said: "I do not think that I am your father, your father will always be Rubio, even knowing that it was not your father, he always loved her very much. Even though I knew it wasn't her father, he always loved sincerely. I wanted to be a worthy man and respected by society, but I was a coward before God. I was a rotten man of spirit, heartless for God. I made a slave of my own daughter, the love of a father you always had, but not a decent home. What I was left to do was to leave all this to you and Manuel, and may God bless you and forgive me.

A few days later, the will was opened, and the Colonel's assets were divided equally to Fabricio and Helen. Fabricio stayed with the Blue Moon farm, where the Colonel had a store in Rio, at street Bossa— on the corner with the wider street. The Colonel had ordered the logo enlarged and next to the lake. The abode made a beautiful house and more... the shops of Barela Street, the church hall, which she donated to the church, an apartment in Lisbon and more, the jewels of Dona Amelia.

The days went by, the romance of Helen, as black daughter of the servant with the son of Colonel Machado changed. Now the people spoke of the Coronel's children, how would it be now? Were they going to be siblings or friends? The people wanted to know.

11

For my great grandparents, they were more than brothers--the passion continued. For the church they could not stay anymore and they also knew that they could not be intimate. Helen confessed that the love she felt for Fabricio was not only brotherly love, the same thing Fabricio had said when confessing to priest Abílio. God must fix the situation.

Often letters arrived to Helen and Fabricio. The people said, "My children, God punishes the recklessness of the home; you must love one another as brothers and sisters, you cannot be married, you can never have children, and every day the same thing was written by the people who lived in Marjara.

On a beautiful Sunday, at the invitation of priest Abílio, Helen and Fabricio went to Mass for the first time together, they did not know that the sermon was for them to give up living together. The Mass began, the priest said: "My brothers, especially the young Hele and Fabricio." The church was full, there were people standing everywhere.

The priest began, "We were all worried about you..." the priest spent an hour and twenty minutes saying that it would be a sin and God would not bless the couple. No longer restraining herself in silence, my great grandmother desperately went to the altar weeping, asked for a minute of silence and peace. She said, "I am left with only the goodness of God. I am three months pregnant and God has to bless my son who was not to blame for anything. "Three months ago I loved Fabricio as a woman in love and Fabricio, too, and we did not know anything.

If God blesses this son and he is born perfect, we will live together. Fabricio, did not know of Helen's pregnancy. His reaction was very emotional and he went to the altar and asked, kneeling, that God would bless them, that priest Abílio would help them to live without worry, and that the people would pray for their son to be born perfect. He declared, "If God gives us this perfect son, me and Helen will take care of him, we will be a family."

Fabricio at this moment took the hands of Helen and looking into the eyes next to the priest and next to the image of Christ and in the moment, they swore that if the child was born perfect, they would be a couple—never separate again... They hugged, the tears fell, and everyone took notice and left, meekly, even the priest left and for a few hours they remained in the church.

The months of 1943 passed quietly and it was a great peaceful moment for the statue of Christ the Redeemer's consecration. It was prayed and gifted for my great grandmother too. Her pregnancy did not bring even one problem. In the ninth month of pregnancy, on June 22, Helen felt that the child would be born. With no time to take her to the hospital, my great grandfather hurried to get the best doctors.

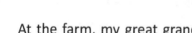

At the farm, my great grandfather's son was in a hurry to be born, and Helen asked to call the midwife—the same one who helped her to be born. The midwife was old. I was just waiting for death, but made a point of going to the Blue Moon farm to see Helen's child after birth. My great grandmother calmly had a perfect and normal birth. And suddenly the baby began to cry, and the midwife commented that the child had mighty lungs. Even with Fabricio's speed, little Andrew, that should be his first name.

That already was in the world, waiting for his father, next to his mother. When my great grandfather arrived, the tears came together and the happiness was so great that he forgot to see if it was boy or girl...didn't bother to ask.

Fabricio said, "I see, my God, it's a boy," and he watched the hands, the little fingers, everything to see if it was perfect.

"God has blessed this family."

In 2017, I did my ethnicity inheritance to figure out who I am and from what stock I originated. A literary worked hard to learn details about the romance of my ancestors going back to my great great-grandparents. The day of the meeting, the address he had in his hands was the same as the Blue Moon farm--of course, a little more modern. My grandfather was waiting for me.

I was enchanted by the beauty of the farm, and most impressed by the care by which my ancestors preserved the ancient things that belonged to great-great-grandparents and grandparents. And near the forest there was a huge stone, carried by the blacks and with the help of Rubio we placed. We then spent hours talking. Luis needed to talk about a project to enlarge the lake. When he was a boy, his grandmother , said that this lake should be bigger. When she rode a boat ride it was short, because the logo was small: - I asked, "How is it to be the great granddaughter of Rubio Andrade and be the great granddaughter colonel Machado? And Fabricio still being Machado's great-grandson?

At twenty-seven years old, Lara said, "I am interested in the things of the city. I try to discover the mysteries of this farm; every corner tells me one thing...reveals a mystery. On this stone that you are leaning, my great grandfather wrote: "I love you, Helen, as you can see, the letter represents a boy who was learning to write. And I said, "Yes, I imagine!

RISK MARKED

12

I started to visit the Blue Moon farm more often, and especially my old cousin, who possessed a better knowledge about our generation. My family's story is not so simple, many changes and many surprises and disagreements.

For the past few years, I had spoken with my cousin only about our age group—how each one of us reacted about our ancestries. "You," my cousin said, "you are the daughter of a good man who helped build this city. But he also lost everything. Your father always will be remembered as a strong man and honest, when you compare to his older brother. Your father had been so good, and he always demanded the truth and his presence exhibited respect, so to be entirely clear, you should not blame your father."

I said, "No, I do not blame my father for anything."

I know about all the fraud. A friend of mine told me about it, and I was surprised that it seemed as if everyone knew already." That was my judgment. It should be with us at the moment, and I do not blame my father. He took his responsibility.

"I need to tell you something."

My cousin said, "Go ahead."

"You know the man who took his life was my father's brother."

"Yes," I said.

I was not allowed to place attention on these issues when I was growing up, and the man who took his life, I thought, was a closer friend of the family. One day I asked my mother about this, and she said, "It's a conversation that we shouldn't have now."

So, I waited until ten years later to know the truth from my father's words. So, his brother sat down to a trade negotiation with the mafia, and told my father that he wanted to get out of the gang. – That's how my father learned the word, "GANG." The Mafia knew that my father knew everything. My father combined all the money he had, and the plan was set. So, the Mafia wanted to kill his brother. My father set everything up and planned for the money, arranged to meet his brother later. But when he got there, he found his brother's body on the floor; he'd gunshot himself.

"I didn't know the gun belonged to my father, and my father gave the money for his brother, made the negotiation, and advised him to meet the Mafia leader." So, these things relate to why my father felt guilty about his brother's death. And, I understood how he must deal with these issues and how he tried all the time to make, and give us straight advice about all things first, see all the possibilities, and in a safe way get out of any situation, or better to not get into. Felipe said with a tremulous voice, "I am his son. He left me behind."

I was so sad to hear this from his heart, with tears coming from his eyes and his face, his eyes were red, and were empty of love. And I remembered the day I confronted my father and aloud I said, "I do not want your advice." And I was sure I hurt his feelings very much.

"Well," I said, "Felipe, usually I receive information from the wrong people or I can say, from someone in the family that shows more drama and more lies interspersed in the information,"

He answered, "Yes, I know what you mean."

During my visits that took hours and hours, we talked a lot. I said, "Felipe, I am the daughter of a man who gave everything for his family." Every day was a day with all special things, but also with some weird, curious facts, that my siblings and many relatives and I wanted to know. And I wanted to know from my parents and from my older sisters, not from the other relations where sometimes the history came from one side only.

I asked my cousin, "How did you hear from your father?"

He said, "The first history I had, the uncles and your father were there and wanted to make the negotiation between both of them." And your father at one point didn't arrive.

"Then everybody thought that your father set this up," and he said, "but one person's testimony did not prove anything. Still some wanted to blame your father."

"Well," I said, "now everyone knows the truth, and I do not understand why people still will not face it."

My cousin answered, "Those kinds of people we should avoid. You understand why, don't you?".

I went on telling my cousin stories about my father's trips. I glanced at my mother's eyes and glimpsed fear and surprise. As for the time, I did not wish to know. I do not want to attempt defending my actions because I think they originated with father or my extractions from the past. When I grew enmeshed I would sometimes stay focused on my feelings. I catalogued all the facts and stories in my heart and mind, so I could think about my own feel-ings. I do believe miracles happen, but you must de-velop a vision based on your own reality. This habit helped me experience different things and be in dif-ferent places at different times. Thus I believe in vi-sion and visualization because it nurtures the desire to live forever.

Finally, I give the impression that I am not fol-lowing my own desires and not backing down all the time saying, "It's a family ... Is it normal... or is it NOT?

I come from a generation of many conflicts and marked risks. I was very scared not knowing how it could affect me and how I took on this responsibility about my great great-grandmothers and great-grand-fathers after birth. This is not a conversation that we normally spoke at home until today. This is the story of my great-grandparents a powerfully affected gen-eration, raised up around many risks in life.

With the passage of years, I've suffered physical discomfort and constant pain due to my injuries and illnesses from generational disease. Time revealed research procedures and later diagnostic insight re-garding some kind of disease that you never hear of. To me, not knowing exactly what happened to my parents brought a lot of discomfort and psychologically troubling modes of behavior. I grew up in the midst of acute social and economic risks from my parents and a loss of confidentiality for what I became.

All around me crashed waves from the sea and it distracted me in my search for relief. I often think of a typical day at the honey island dunes on beaches, a rough sea, strong winds and a lot of heat. These adjectives seem to sum up the summers of my life.

At twelve years of age, I remembered that not far from the beautiful beaches near the island of honey, I wrote my name on a beach. No one liked to go there, because it was a deserted beach, but it was where I liked to go, especially at night. There the beach was beautiful by the light of the moon... that was the most beautiful, I thought, and it was not only me who liked this beach. There was another who loved and communed with the sea; it was the t was the moon at midnight. The moon felt lost in love and happy as if it imagined itself rolling across the sand now and then, immersed in the salty sea. I was excited for the sea; it seemed like a living thing. And then, before I ran away, I watched the two of them kissing, the sea and the moon. I imagined how beautiful it would be to see my parents loving each other like that.

With the passage of years, I eventually baptized

the new beach, naming it the beach of the living moon. In the several years that I lived on the beach, waves crashing, moon rising, I witnessed and lived some very sad moments of abuse from my cousin. It was sort of like a stupid death and at the same time I was periodically reborn again.

When I met Mariana, my new friend, I remembered the day--May 11 at the parking lot of the school. I always memorized dates of events. Often I did not want to remember, because life felt to me very cold and wind-driven.

Rain punished nature, punished life. I saw Mariana going to school, but the school was a little bit too far from the island. In the first three months I saw Mariana every day at the bus stop, then I noticed Mariana was not often coming to school, though at the time I did not place much importance on her disappearance. I was in love with Francisco, my friend, and he seemed to like me.

I wanted to forget the abuse, but sometimes I did not want to forgive my cousin. These clashing emotions so confused my feelings. On the weekends I didn't run away alone to the beach of the living moon. It was me and Francisco, but I was afraid of being abused even though I liked him. Francisco tried to leave me, but the sea whispered in the moon's ear just as Francisco was trying to whisper in my ear.

13

Every night, it could be cold or hot, we never left the sea alone and neither did the moon. For some particular reason the moon would disappear for a few moments, a day, or for several days, and the sea would be sad, just as I was because Francisco always traveled to Portugal to see his great-grandfathers. I imagined the sad sea weeping without the moon, and so the days passed. Breaking up with Francisco was sad and without explanation. He went to visit his relative in Portugal, and he never returned. When he arrived at Portugal, he always called. Suddenly this ended. For many years, I wondered about what happened to him. I had no more news and when I went to his parents' house in the same city that I lived, there was no one living there anymore. Very strange, but to calm myself, I always took a long walk. I tried to do some different things that kept me busy. I signed up to play volleyball. I forced myself to take a hot soothing bath for long hours, not an easy way to relieve the stress, specially if I was at my parents' house.

Even though Francisco knew that though I didn't constantly show that I was completely in love with him, I did cared very much for him. And I thought, "It is not fair what he's doing. Surely he still wants to be part of my life and he knows this." I always was very mature and I understood his job and his trips with his family in a way that showed that I was relaxed. The night before Francisco left for his trip, I assumed he was at his place—very close to me. He called me, but said nothing about going somewhere or even planning a trip.

And I said, "Francisco, do you see the Moon tonight? It may remind you of our first weekend a few years ago—our first trip together."

And he said, very joyfully, "Yes, and every day I hope we can have many of those great weekends."

He was very present, and I hadn't the faintest clue that the next day he would disappear. I thought, Francisco looks like he cares about me. We have known each other for years and been together for less than two years, but it is not about time. It is about feelings that had found my way into Francisco's heart. I caught his kiss and held it next to my heart.

Back to old days, my father never took a steaming shower. First, because energy came at a higher price and second, he always said a hot shower would make your skin feel dry and you'd look older sooner. I always laughed.

I was not very interested in reading an interesting book or magazine, but I loved writing plays. Calling a friend to talk was not an option. and striking up a conversation also was not on my schedule.

The following year, I went to Biru Ipe, already twenty-two years old and still in love with Francisco. Going out with my friends gave me an opportunity to meet different guys. But Francisco seemed to act like the world without him would end; the beaches all resembled Francisco. They were not like my living beach. The days passed and I had to change my life and look for another direction to live. The sea was like that with tides flowing in and out. I cried until we finished the vacation. Soon I returned to honey island. I felt something strange when I arrived, but finally I recognized it as feelings of distress and worry.

I tried to call Francisco again that afternoon. Of course, he didn't answer. I asked myself why he'd disappeared from me and never called at work either. Why would he do that? The next day I called at his workplace, and his coworkers said that his file showed a notation that he was supposed to come back to work in two weeks. And two weeks had already passed.

"Listen," the coworker said, "maybe you can ask his neighbor about him?"

"Yes, that's a good idea, I should do that."

However, next day before going to Francisco's neighbor, I called Mariana for advice. I knew Mariana would give me some advice to help me find my man.

Mariana knew Francisco, and she shared her view about him.

"Hello Mariana, can we meet?"

"Yes," she said.

We met at a coffee shop by the Church at the main park of the town.

I was working on my breathing–in and out. After a general conversation about work and college, I finally asked Mariana, "How long have you known Franscisco?"

She said, "I know Franscisco through my cousin; they usually get together on the weekend to play soccer."

"I thought you knew him a long time ago,"

"Not really, I met him maybe two weeks or less before you."

I closed my eyes.

And Mariana asked me, "What happened? Tell me."

"Something sad maybe has happened with Francisco."

Mariana paused. "Franscisco?" she said, "yes, he went to Portugal for a vacation for a couple weeks and never returned—not even a letter or phone call, I think that he hates me or he died and no one from his family knows about me."

"What? No. I don't believe that he could do that."

"Then why didn't he return from his work?"

"I remember ... he always said how much he liked his work and the new position that he was promoted to before his trip. And he told me that he could also apply for a new position soon. And I always encouraged him you know, Mariana. I saw his father once, and his mother. I didn't ever remember her face, and he didn't offer much encouragement to take me to visit his family. I didn't care much about that either. And I was so happy to have him that I didn't want to complain about getting to know his family. They looked completely indifferent and it seems that they wanted Francisco to have a different girlfriend."

"Well," Mariana said, "yes, he is a lovely man, and he should contact you as soon he gets there."

"But he didn't and he never did that before; he

always sent messages every day throughout his trip, and his parents always traveled with him to Portugal. Mariana asked, "The house is closed? No one there? You have to contact his landlords or someone else?"

"Yes," I said, "that's why I'm here."

"Okay. Tell me what you need. I can't stand here and do nothing to learn what happened to him."

"Yes, I agree."

"It's true that Franscisco and you never travel together?"

I said, "No. not true, we went to Canada once. Just the two of us. Not his family. He liked to travel with his family, but always they came back on the exact day they planned. There was something not clear. I guess I just needed to get his family information about his new life. One moment I could think, the next was unclear in my mind. What should I do, Mariana? Do you think I should travel to Portugal?"

She was thinking. "No, you should stay here and try to talk to his neighbor," she said. "You shouldn't put yourself in a difficult and expensive situation. I was about to ask Mariana if she would be coming with me, and she already was giving me an answer." But, I said, "well, it will be more difficult to know what happened if I stay here."

"Maybe you, should not know what happened, and if I was you, I'd try very hard to either forget

Francisco or see who knows him and his family. You should stop being so worried, and you should stop calling him."

"I know, Mariana! I realize I should stop thinking about him! And I've given so many explanations to my family about him. I lied about all that because I really didn't know what happened to him and his family. I called a million times already."

Mariana said, "Why don't you call the operation and give this number?"

"The number you have; you talked to him before, that is correct? Yes, I got the number from him and I called before and he answered all the time. I should go to his neighbor later today or tomorrow.

I tried so hard to speak with that neighbor but he didn't want to give me information, saying, "Miss Lara Alberene, I don't know anything. I just know that the house is empty. I opened the house two days ago with permission, and the house was empty. That's the only thing I can tell you."

The neighbor said, "Be careful."

I said, "What do you mean?"

"I think you should not come here anymore." The neighbor added, "I have seen you around the house many times. And you need to move on."

"Forget it," he said. "Erasing things in your life—sometimes that is the one thing we need to do."

There was a long moment of silence as I figured out how to respond.

"Forgetting …. intimate memories and feelings?" I said. "It's not an easy process."

Mariana had been waiting in silence all this time. She said, "Just let me to talk to the neighbor, and try to understand feelings that haven't been given the right answer yet!" Mariana continued, "You thought that you could be so convincing that you would easily get the information that you wanted."

Mariana had the same luck in reasoning with the landlord as I did—none!. After Francisco and his family's disappearance, I was recalling him saying that in the future his family wanted to move back to Portugal, because they wanted to stay closer to their relatives, and wanted to travel more to Germany. I didn't figure it would happen anytime soon, but I didn't ask when this could happen. I had the impression that Francisco would stay in Brazil, as he'd become successful here and his family was very good! They had excelled, shall we say. I'd struggled for answers and tried to get people's attention for months. I had been searching and looking for information about Francisco. Then I realized that he was truly gone and the family had melted away like a snowman in springtime.

And yes, I had accepted my feelings and worries

and I needed to forget all of them in order to have any peace return to my heart. And I had to try to forgive Francisco who had broken my heart in fragments as a result of this fake relationship and after months, I finally moved on for good. Well, now, I saw things move more toward my direction.

I know the reality. Francisco moved and he wasn't at home anymore. But I would be happy to be able to see him again or hear some news about him.

Early August, beginning of classes, on the first day a surprise. Who did I see at the bus stop? It was Mariana, different, long hair pricked and painted. I found it strange but she was extra kind and said to me that she needed a friend. She had entered into some very cold and deep waters and so for that reason she had disappeared from school. Also, she lied to her grandmother. She had told her grandmother that she was going to make a two-month excursion outside Brazil. "My poor grandmother," Mariana said, "I lied to my grandmother who took care of me since my parents died when I was five years old. Today, I am twenty-three and still lost."

I asked Mariana about how her parents died.

She said, "They were driving to the farm that my

father had bought; my mother and brother went to-gether too, but the car fell into the rushing river and my brother's body was not found. I learned that only my father and mother were buried.

"Oh! I did know that you had a brother; sorry."

Mariana said, "I spent a lot of time playing with my brother. His name was Duda. He was six years older than I. I stayed at home on that day because I was very sick. My brother and I used to play every day in the backyard for hours until Dad came home from work. Dad had a lot of business and also want-ed to be mayor of the city."

Mariana's father was involved in things related to political issues. In 1976, Brazil was renamed the Republic of the United States of Brazil to Federative Replace of Brazil with so many conflicts. Mariana said, "I remembered my father so upset with the re-gime in Brazil with the brutalization of the policy." And my father always remembered that his friend's son died because of the policy because his son was in protest for cheaper prices at a restaurant for low-income students. That moment scarred the dictator-ship, period."

"Now," she said, "how dirty were the politics back then. I loved my father, but now," she said, "Lara, I tried to remember only the good things he did, but my mother I missed her enormously. I completely

understood, that my friend, Mariana, always wanted to go to heaven to find her parents ever since she
was seven years old.

We became friends and many of our memories
are tied together. She said, "Your cousin usually
came and we played together. At first, it was very
good, your cousin, Alfonso played with me every
day, you remember. Then one day I choked when
Alfonso's name was mentioned. I wanted not to talk
about him. I never forgot that he called me to play in
the yard, but he wanted to touch me in my private
parts, improperly. I was very bothered by this situation, but I never said anything and when Mariana
started talking about him, I changed the subject,
very wounded and embarrassed. Mariana changed
the subject but I continued to talk about her disappearance, her attempted suicide. And Mariana said,
"Anyway, I'm here still alive as you see!"

Back then, didn't I tell anyone about my cousin Alfonso? Likely it was because I didn't want to
shame myself by telling about the things he did to
Mariana and to me. When he had the accident, the
police came afterward to talk to everyone who were
with him that day: Mariana, Paula, Roberto, Carla,
Ricardo, Francisco and I. What the police wanted to

know was if anyone had a problem with Alfonso and if anything unusual happened during that day. All the interrogation was straightforward and seemed that all the discussions were very interesting from the officers' point of view.

First, I thought that I should tell the truth, but if I did it might be a red flag and I could become the main suspect, even though I was feeling relief that he was hurt. Then we learned later about his death and still later about his dirty past. I did not know before he died that he was beginning to traffic children as sex slaves. I know because Francisco's father's friends mentioned it. I assumed if he did die, it would be in jail. If a man goes to jail for abuse related to children automatically his jail mates called "friends" would kill him. That's what they do in prison, and they deserve it. I had never thought that he should be given a second chance.

When he did his cliff-jumping, the police said, "It was a miracle, and according to hospital records, there was a possibility that he couldn't walk anymore, and he ended up with a bow-legged lurch. However less than a year after the accident, as was mentioned, he got a cancer and suffered but never anywhere or in any situation did he ask for forgiveness, and I believe that he even thought he didn't do anything wrong. Maybe as he was dying he may have selfishly been feeling sorry for himself. "WHY ME"? But that is life, Sometimes we humans think this way: "We are good persons, and we have done good a few times. We give a lot of reasons for us to receive mercy and we forget the bad ones."

And, I felt like I was not a good person, because I was afraid to tell the truth, to make him to stop, because I lied, and I was continuing to lie and to tell a good history about my life. But I had a place in my heart that was not good, nor was it safe. Those were the crazy thoughts I had when I stopped and Analise my cousin lost his life.

The police called my name. It was my time to be joined with Mariana and both could tell the truth about him. I saw the opportunity to tell the truth, I remembered how I'd been so anxious, and most of the time, I was afraid and I did not want to feel guilty about the accident, even though I was very joyful (GOD FORGIVE ME). And also, I was not ready to deal with all the feelings and to know exactly what happened. One day Mariana said to me that she didn't want life in the same space and real world that she would see or hear from Alfonso." And, she confessed to me what happened. Then she started saying that she asked this guy, she never told me who it was, but she paid for him to do something symbolic. One night they moved many rocks and many boulders to the exact spot where Alfonso always jumped many times for many years and he knew that no rocks were there.

I knew," but she added, "I didn't care very much, and I was thinking more about the safety of many children that he would have abused.

I was only seventeen, and feeling that he would learn a lesson, coming from a family that gave an excuse for anyone's actions, and also, I saw that was the one way the family could be conceived and I said, "It was fate. It had to be like that, not due to responsibility or choices that were made." I locked myself into a bookshelf, waiting for someone to open it and read and ask questions.

Time passed and I see as if from far away that this happened. With all the attitudes and weird junk, I said to myself, "I am stuck in complications of my own making because I'm in denial. Not having the courage to tell the truth."

Mariana metaphorically told the police that she had never had any problem with Alfonso.. She felt too down and sad to admit what occurred. I knew that she wouldn't tell the truth, and how it would become difficult to her daily life with her own responsibility of coming clean regarding what actually happened. Thus, following her example, the means to uncover all the abuse disappeared as years dragged by.

For a long time I hated the fact that we declined being strong together and telling the truth, and I know for a long time she hated me for presenting her to my cousin. "It was a way to escape; in this way he could be interested in her instead of me?" I thought he would do that because he already had a real girlfriend. I thought that I deserved good things, and once again it has happened in my family, and the cycle continues. When would I be strong enough to break the deadly patterns?

Finally for the first time in my life, I had the courage to break this cycle. I was nobody yet, until I made a long trip inside myself to allow me to understand and devote the time to process all these issues and be honest. I found myself before not giving a real analysis and putting there all the frustrations, the lies in my family, and the nonsensical information. After all the investigation and reports, I read the final rendering. It stated that the accident was closed and everything was cleared related to the accident. I realized that Mariana didn't do the right thing in not telling the truth. If I told the police what I knew, both of us would be in very serious complications. And so many denunciations with false ideas would be involved and would remain in our lives forever, and I knew the police and the detectives wouldn't care about us. They just wanted to solve any crime even without deep knowledge, but with shallow agreement. They wanted everyone to sign a paper. Obviously, I would tell the truth, but the questions were not there as to whether he was a good guy or not. The question was if someone pushed him.

So, the point was not helping Alfonso, but yes ... my point was supporting Mariana and myself. And I would be doing damage to us now. But again, I was pretending that everything was over, and life would go on down a smooth path. Every day, things were proven, as if I had an accident, and I thought it should be this way. Sometimes a matter wasn't related to a family cycle. I would say "so sorry," to myself. No behaviors from inherited attitudes should ever be reported as an excuse for your own behavior.

Shortly after all these chaotic and disorganized police interrogations, I left for an interview to work at a Lab in this new company that just opened in Sao Paulo. It was the kind of job that fit me and I was very interested to be part of the Lab. I said to

Mariana, "You should apply for a new position that's opening pretty soon."

And she said, "The terrible thing that I did, I still feel that I don't know me, and it has upset me now knowing that he is dead. I neglected to tell the truth when he was alive and did not confront him and hear him humble himself and apologize." The existence of the real fact, the feeling of the damage was still there and had not been answered and understood. I felt as if we only brushed on a coat of varnish over the truth.

Mariana was trying to explain to me that she could not move forward without telling the real truth. And she explained, "It's like I'm an ice rock; it seems strong when I am in a cold place.. "But," Mariana added, "as the ice melts I see myself running like water. I can't get out of these daydreams that bring me embarrassment and worries that something will happen to me. I will never be able to tell the true story. But I don't care any more to confess that I ordered others to move rocks from the edge and throw them at the perfect spot. I also want to say that I lost my baby because of him." Finally and, Mariana, said "I just wanted to tell that Afonso was a bad person and he deserve to die."

And then a month later we went to camping to get out of the social median and the city was in the headlines and a lot of the news was about the Alfonso accident. No one was guilty, so we needed a time to relax and talk between us, and see if we can figure out what really happened. Mariana and I wanted this case to reach complete closure. I came to Alfonso's funeral. I had to be respectful to my aunt, but I didn't understand when she said, "Alfonso's had so many problems, just like his grandfather."

Oh! I hated to hear that. I heard so many of these comments in my family, saw some of them doing things and blaming the "Family Cycle."

Once again I whispered, "No, don't count me in on this ugly excuse for the truth."

You can see that family resemblance attached easier, and it sometimes brought comfort that only extended skin-deep. I knew this situation, and this I couldn't handle. I often saw my body in this box, but before I put my head in, I let the beautiful moon wake me up before the sunlight began filtering through the trees. I saw myself out of my self-imposed box and walking away to define my reality and define myself. That is the life, and it is an unsettled move to be able to get off the chest the heavy thoughts. Those are the encounters that you need. I understood.

14

I asked Mariana how she had attempted suicide. She said, "I lived in an apartment, on the fifth floor, me and my grandparents. I was in my room when my grandmother called me for lunch and I was at the window looking down, when suddenly it came to my head the huge desire to meet my mother, and these memories hit a huge depression and at that moment I was falling apart. When I sat on the base of the window to throw myself down, my grandmother entered the room, and I slipped and fell. My grandmother came running desperately, did not even want to wait for the elevator to come back. She ran to the nervous staircase and slipped, toppling down the stairs, arriving at the ground floor motionless. She was taken to the hospital along with me."

Mariana stopped talking a little and began

crying, her tears like a raining...a cleansing. Her face became so red that not even the tears extinguished the fire of her face. I also cried a lot with her. I said, "How can we ever erase all this from our minds?"

It seemed that everyone around knew what happened; everyone was telling about it. Mariana said, "Once I heard family members complain and blame me about my grandmother. Mariana added, "I heard lots of conversation about my option to go to a convent." After my parents died, I had attempted suicide. "That was the word flying around. But then you must know my grandmother..."

When we got to the hospital, grandmother was quite bruised. I didn't see anything, only after some days could I see the sun. When I could talk I asked for grandma,

"Where's Grandma and why did she not come to visit me yet?"

Later, Mariana learned that her grandma had fallen down the stairs and broken her spine, and as she had chronic back stiffness already, the accident caused serious problems in her life. "She who took me to school, she who drove Mom's car, she who taught me to swim in the summer, and grandma woke up super early—like 5:00 in the morning for her walking. Now she couldn't do those things anymore. After her walking, she'd made a delicious orange juice. "When it was on the weekends, we both went shopping or to some local farms."

"Today," Mariana said, "after nine years, I see grandma in the wheel working. This hurts me and makes me feel very sad, so I decided to disappear as soon as grandma got better. I talked to her and she thought it best if I could travel, but I was not to travel far. When I left, Mariana said, "I was very close. I rented a room in the countryside. I didn't want to return to my house. It contained a lot of things that reminded me of my parents. My parent's house is very much closer to my grandparents; almost every day we were there for lunch or dinner. Mariana said, "After my mother got a job at the pharmacy, my brother and I were at my grandparents' every day after school." She continued, "They loved walking us to school. My father always went away for a couple days of business, but he always came back exactly on the day he said he would return."

She spoke as if in a dream, "I saw my parents describe each other in a beautiful word garden, comprehensive with love and respect." I saw Mariana's eyes fill with tears and she went outdoors looking for a peaceful moment."

But everything changed after I started hanging out with your cousin. That was a huge mistake... When my brother died, she said, "Alfonso, took over my brother's space; you remember that he was always with us. So, my brother gone, he would come to my grandparents' house almost every day to play with me in the yard and do weird things, but I missed my brother, and Alfonso, tried to be my big brother. Because I was no longer by myself, Alfonso had the same pranks as my brother, and I thought that I was safe." And Mariana said, "I missed my brother, and Alfonso said, that he was here for me. The conversation was interrupted because Mariana said, "I want to forget everything he did and all the people who were around me."

Once Mariana explained about 'prescription' drugs which were rather new at the time. "People gave her drugs that almost killed her. "It wasn't them entirely, but rather the damn drug I thought was pure magic." And she said, "I was thinking that a drug makes it possible to never get sick and see a doctor."

On those days, I look at every aspect of my life and I realize what Mariana said, "The whole time I was attached to myself. I humiliated my own dignity for being around Alfonso, I endangered my own life, and I let my sleep time die, choked by sad feelings and uncomfortable thoughts, I wouldn't sleep."

I was surprised and in shock, and I could feel Mariana's pain. Mariana was telling me about her brother, and she said one day, "My brother thinks you are cute,"

I said, "You never said your brother came here to play because of me."

And then she said, "Maybe, I don't know."

Anyway, I don't remember being asked about her family much after that. As kids we used to play outside, especially in the summer, until it got dark, but we didn't worry much about going inside, until my father mentioned the oft-repeated horror story, and everyone get scared and panicked, ran for the house.

Mariana hated to talk about her childhood partly because she grew up without her mother. The only reason she is alive was because she and her grandmother survived the accident, but she felt guilt even after seeing her grandmother survive.

Mariana, I asked, "What makes you feel so guilty? Your grandmother survived the fall pretty well."

Mariana said, "I was supposed to clean the stairs and move all the things like my shoes and the basket of clothes. My grandmother asked me to do this earlier. It was my job since I was a little girl. We lived on the second floor; we had always lived in houses with stairs and that was my chore in the house; it was commonly everyone's living things on the stairs, and that day I forgot. It was my biggest mistake and I cried."

Mariana said, "The night before, I was planning to kill myself. All the feelings, all the questions in my mind had no answer."

I listened and thought: That is so sad and how you look after me all this time. I was looking at everyone's faces and all were strangers to me.

Perhaps Mariana was trying to find her questions and believed that she could find answers to by lifting these questions up to the sky. I asked her again about her brother's never recovering. I felt miserable after I asked her these questions. I felt uncomfortable, and that finished my questions for the day.

Mariana started screaming that she didn't want to go back to live with her old friends that used drugs and alcohol to minimize the pain. She wanted to be different, and she wanted to start with her hair--this ugly, dirty hair. On this day we didn't go to school, maybe on this day we became friends again. I went to the saloon to cut Mariana's hair. I asked for help, but sometimes when you try to help someone without asking, it can be a problem. Anyway, I knew Mariana would get free hair color and nail polish. Mariana placed her hands in the car door which was broke, and tried to open the door so hard that she broke her fingernails. For a few minutes she was in pain so bad that she proceeded to say such a string of profane words my grand's mouths popped open.... It hurt a lot.

I was concerned that she wouldn't want to go to the salon anymore. She said, "Wait a minute; I forgot my purse. Would you please pay for me?" She told me what the approximate price would be.

I said, "Yes, no problem." After manicure and pedicure and hair was done, we went back to the house. I remembered the car door would be very hard to open. And I said, "Please open nice and slow."

Mariana had so much hatred of her hair that she asked to cut it very short. Her mother usually did her hair, and then later her grandmother, but both were not present anymore in her life. So, after the hair was done, she felt free and as her hair grew back she started to recognize herself again.

That afternoon, she returned to her grandmother's house with her bags and happy to have such a wonderful grandparent who loved her so much. Mariana's return made her grandmother very happy.

The months rushed by quickly. I couldn't get through school properly. I was trying to recover in math. I left for college and Mariana was a year late, but the important thing was to go back to school and make new friends. Mariana said, "I've always been no good at math and geography; those subjects I don't get. We were in the last year of high school and the graduation party would be a tour of Fernando de Noronha. The anxiety of passing was great; next year we would all move and attend college. It would be great if we were all together: Mariana, Lucia Paulo, Roberto, Lucia, Ricardo and especially, Francisco.

I told her, "You know, Mariana, since we became friends, you know all my secrets. I never want to lie to you because I feel that I need to trust someone, and you came into my life like an angel. Everyone else didn't want to be serious and supportive. I'd turn out to be a different person after being transferred to a new office and I'd get more serious about college. I didn't pass the first time; I needed to grow up and be more responsible.

I loved to be with the group and do things all together. I was empty after the exams, I went back home and my parents didn't respond well to my return. They thought that I should apply myself and get better grades. I should get a better score compared to all the rest of the group because I had all the best preparation. My family did everything to pay for my preparation courses to get into the best university. My father did an extra service on the weekends to bring more money into the house. Now all these hardworking days were for nothing. And I'd look at them and think, I was so idiotic to be involved with Francisco and all his friends. How did this happen? How did I finally pass on the exams? I was just a girl full of love and everyone was feeling the same.

Still interested, I went back to talk to Mariana, and I said, "Some of my family's traditional stories with no offense, should live the lifespan of a dragon-fly (no offense), so I couldn't hear for so many years relatives bringing up the past that interfered with my present in a way I didn't like."

She said, "I'm understanding that my grandparents are the same way, and if my parents were not dead I am sure they would act the same."

And I said, "Is there such a thing as a relatively normal family cycle. For me it molted my behavior, mixed my ability to understand my attitude, and Lucia was around too and spoke for me, "Family wisdom finally gave me opportunity to breathe to my own cadence, capture my own thoughts, and help me peel back my own experience quickly, because I had the ability to understand my family knowledge--their insight." And I sort of understood Lucia's point of view.

And I said, "Holding a dragonfly? Maybe you don't have the time that should be necessary to resolve any kind of feelings that are attached to a big wound, and apparently I will not grow much happiness if I live worrying over every little thing.

Since Mariana and Lucia arrived last night from a Parana to attend a meeting at Sao Paulo, we had been together. They invited us to have lunch and go shopping afterward.

I asked," If they want to stay at my place, plan of room was very happy that they said yes.

And Mariana said, "Does your brother know that you invited me?"

I said, "Don't worry. He has changed a lot and has been very nice, and every time he had a chance to talk, he says sorry even though he knows I live with his girlfriend. And I said, "He doesn't really care anymore; he seems very relaxed, guys." We laughed a lot and Lucia said, "His girlfriend has been doing a good job."

"Mariana," I said, "do you remember Paulo,

Francisco's cousin. It surprised me that she mentioned his name, because Paulo was stupid with most girls and he did not seem to care much about feelings. I really thought that he was a spoiled brat without respect toward anyone. At the time I remember nobody seemed to like the guy. I was terrified to be around him because, a friend of mine mentioned that he tried to force her to stay with him, and I knew what I wanted to say.

She said, "Yes, I know."

Anyway, I was not good-looking enough for him. Plus, I was clear that I did not like him very much and I was not in the conversations between them most of the time, and of course I had eyes only for Francisco Even though he was not into school at the moment, he couldn't focus on complex topics and had no interest in hard topics. I clearly understood that he had a problem with learning. I wondered whether there was any connection with his sister. He sacrificed too much. Every time he saw his parents they only talked about his twin baby sister, who honestly, the parents thought, was abducted. They still believed that they would find her one day. It seemed that the baby girl may conceivably be alive somewhere, and that one day they'd all be together like a lovely family with the baby girl.

After the disappearance of Francisco, his family

rushed to Germany for a year. Basically, his explanation was that they went to find his twin sister but he could not say anything about it. I imagine how hard it was to love someone you never knew, not even knowing how she looked! But I believe that they would be alike. And Dona Isabel would recognize her sameness very quickly.

Before Francisco left, one day I kind of remember he mentioned that his family asked for many hospitals to research, and asked to review all the hospital files to see if any girl was born there about twenty years ago, and to check for possible DNA to prove that the baby really was dead.

Francisco said, "We gave all the time and money necessary to reach an outcome. For the family this examination did not bring any positive result. No, they knew that a baby born during that period had DNA that matched the family. This result gave my parents hope and they were surely optimistic because they believed that my twin baby sister might yet be alive. I dreamed and tried to hear all the conversation about Francisco's life and his family. It was very sad to know that your own daughter might yet be alive but you couldn't find her.

Francisco said, "Days and days passed as they scoured many cities and towns. They even went to Germany, because the doctor that did the operating at the time was from Germany and also was a family friend. But I thought they needed to look anywhere possible, if they believed the daughter was alive. And I thought it was the right thing to do when you believe that you can bring the person back to you to be part of your life forever.

For a moment I was on my mental journey and soon flipped back to reality, I liked it in my father's house--new job, new friends. I put myself into an international language program, and met many people with the same goal: one day to travel the world. A lot of them wanted to visit a faraway place and return, another wanted the opportunity to leave and not come back. And coming to the class and going out with these friends made me feel important and I had an advantage. I was almost conversational in English and French. I attended the program for two years. This was the time that I needed to make money and come back to try again my dream course. I passed a University Federal of Sao Paulo; I started preparing my bags and things to take with me. The test only takes four days. I did not need many clothes. I had a place already to stay for a few days.

Once I got there, I saw Francisco walking in my direction at the airport, with his little lady Bug. We called it a "Fusco" blue, small but very clean and had enough space for my luggage. I noticed that he seemed uncomfortable as he spent time with his family, struggling with the lack of connection. Yet he tried all the time to be normal and made me feel happy.

We kissed, but didn't move into a full blown romance. My focus was on my goal and I didn't want to fall short again. Maybe we could talk after my exams. I needed this time and this chance to mature and become a biochemical engineer; that was my dream.

"It's completely okay and normal to feel these ways," Francisco said.

I said, "Thank you, and I really hope that you understand that I do love you. All my feelings point me toward living with you and seeing our relationship grow."

After all the moments we had, I had nothing against feelings that supported my love for Francisco.

15

The day of the final exam came, it was a Monday, November 15, 1975. I spent the weekend studying with the help of Francisco. Mariana also had reinforcements in the classes she needed. We did the test quietly, and we waited for the result that would come out five hours later. We managed to pass, the happiness was so palpable that we went to celebrate on the beach: "Living Moon." And then Christmas arrived, and Mariana received a car. It was the biggest gift she ever got, not because it was a simple car, but it was her mother's car. So Mariana's grandmother said, "Mariana needs to learn to live alone; next year she will already be going to college. And on August 20th I turned eighteen and also had to take care of her father's business.

Francisco just arrived from his mother's house the day before the exams. He passed a few days with his parents before he met us. Francisco's mother is a very classically beautiful lady, dressed very well, used only fine jewelry. She wanted Francisco to stay closer to her all the time; it seemed she protected him very much and during his last visit they fought, because she wanted to control his life, and since the beginning I had a problem with her accepting me. She couldn't understand why her son got involved with me, and the worst part is that she knew that we had a brief but very intense relationship before.

Francisco and I had been very close, but for some reason inside it seemed a little confusing. I avoided thinking much about it because again I was wondering, and I was being rejected like my great grandfather. I did not want to think about my past, but it's there and I wondered how I could resolve these feelings and this situation, so I wouldn't live in the past. I do not want to give space for this transmissible birth defect. And I hoped that I would find a way to deal with this; it seemed so real and all-consuming."

But the happiness between me and Francisco, it was a sparkling thing, natural and very joyful. I too had to admit those feelings and completely ignore Francisco's mother's remarks. I had a big bag of trouble as she continually tried to control her son.

Francisco ignored her and always said to his mother, 'Lara had nothing to do with her heritage, as I also had nothing to do with your past." He added, "I need to be aware of my own nest and not think much of the remaining memories that narrow my trail."

Francisco sat by my side and quickly started to talk with other friends, asking, "Any plan after the exams?"

Mariana quickly responded, "No but I thought we were already set to go again to the Eucalypts Beach?"

"Oh yes!" I responded. "We should prepare as soon as possible."

"Who is coming?" Francisco asked.

I said, "In all likelihood, everyone: Roberto, Carlos, Carla, Mariana, Francisco, and me. You all come, that is correct?"

Mariana smiled, and she said, "I'm in."

"Yes," ...for Robert, Carlos, Francisco and I." Mariana said. "How about Paulo, Fabio, and et cetera..,"

I said, "No problem, I believe they are coming too."

I took the responsibility to rent the house and also set the time to pick up the key and deliver payment. I felt that it was my time to check all these things and Francisco said, "May I help you?"

I said, "Yes, of course!"

Carlos got the responsibility to organize things this time and I offered to help, because Carla and Mariana always had to arrange these things, and I wanted to be cooperative this time. I had made myself busy, so I couldn't leave space to carry feelings, that now and then brought tears. But I couldn't clear my thoughts yet.

Finally came the day to travel, as it was agreed to spend the holidays in the Archipelago of Fernando de Noronha. We were inseparable, and most of the time we did our best to be all together. It was the first time we all traveled with Francisco. We loved each other a lot, I know. It was a teenage passion, and the passion never died. But, sometimes our feelings were a bit confused. Was it love with passion or just passion? We stayed in a beautiful house seaside and even had a small boat. That night Paula and Roberto wanted to go out. I remember Roberto's happiness when he learned that Paula would go with us. He always liked Paula, but she was linked to his brother, Thiago. Just the same, Thiago did not want anything to do with ladies; he did not even like to stay with us. He got involved with another man. They had to move out from his house, and he and his partner decided to get married. Paula was disappointed, but she moved on. And she decided to go with us to Fernando de Noronha. For Roberto it was the chance he'd always wanted, he dreamed of the day when he could stay with Paula. During the trip, Roberto revealed his love. Paula decided that she would consider it seriously. After all, Roberto was handsome, green eyes, hair no one could fault, a golden body. Paula began to observe Roberto's mouth, but she was silent. "C'mon! guys, are we going to leave or not?"

Francisco looked at me and his eyes met mine. I could not stop looking at him and he would not stop praising me either.

The next morning Francisco went to my room to wake me up. It was already past ten in the morning, and the sun was already penetrating all the space of the room. He affectionately told me, "My Crystal of Honey, I brought a strawberry juice. I know you like it.

"You know how to make me happy, don't you?"

"You keep pleasing me, saying beautiful words and calling me Crystal."

"Sit here next to me, and take some of this juice, it's delicious."

"Well, the invitation is yours, but I was actually looking forward to getting closer to you."

"Funny but I was thinking that I would always be a star that shone in your life. Yet I was afraid that something would happen and all this, all our love may end.

He said, "Nonsense, I love you."

Francisco asked, "Tell me something; where is the rest of the group?"

"They left very early, went to the other side of the Island, and mingled with the neighbors on that side."

"So, there are only two of us left?"

He said, "Yes, can you move or shift further, so I can lie down with you in this cozy bed?

I moved next to him on the bed, and we were together talking for two hours.

Francisco's arms hugged me very tenderly, his hands were like cotton, but there was a feeling of passion mixed with charm, seduction and at this time as we talked together you were the most attractive person I knew. We had to laugh together because we were suddenly feeling very intimate. After awhile I had to get up because the caresses were enticing us to make love. I got up and took a cold shower, while Francisco made a delicious salad, rice, chips and fish with shrimp sauce. The fish were always caught by us, always fresh, along with a tasty fruit salad with papaya, banana, mango and orange–the fruits I had around to pick from the trees. It was all beautiful and perfect.

After lunch we went to the hammock, which was on the balcony in full view of the sea. I could hear the cadence of the waves and I felt the affection of Francisco's hands, his arms embraced me with great passion, the kisses drove me crazy, and made me want to enter his heart. In his mind and in the intimacy of his world I fell asleep. It was a wonderful feeling those moments of love, and so the afternoon faded serenely into the vastness of the clear sky.

Francisco hugged me tightly in that hammock and with much affection and desire his hands passed over my body, the touches of the gods' fingers lightly closed my eyes and our lips came together. Our moments of caressing were eternal, our voices were so soft that we ended up falling asleep in the hammock for a few hours. When we woke up, the moon had cleared the sky. We remembered our living moon and decided to go boating; we were in no hurry to return, the whole time of the universe was ours. Life was a dream waiting to happen and we saw not a cloud in the sky.

For a moment I remembered, I was frightened that my father would read my eyes. Later that night, in the dark I heard my sisters talking very excited about some news. They were reading a letter about my sister's college acceptance. It made me happy too.

My younger sister wanted to be a pilot, but my mother didn't approve very much. She was so scared of flight. I believed that she never boarded an airplane once. My father and I had some trips together; he always traveled for business.

My conversation with my father at the moment paused, and my sister Cleo was the one who received the attention and she deserved all the attention. It was very cool that she had been accepted into the Air Force program. My sister's acceptance was very important to my father, because that was his dream too. He did not have much support to follow his college path and reach his dream as a pilot. All his money from his hermitage family was gone because they did not pay taxes and the land that my great grandfather bought never belonged to him, because all the papers of agreement that he signed were fake.

He had many pressures to work at a young age. My sisters and I really appreciated our parents' effort to give us the best they could. From the moment

I had to choose my activities at school, my mother was around, giving support and teaching me an easier way to understand and solve problems. But sometimes I couldn't understand because particular subjects could be complicated. Sometimes my sisters said, "You... You worry too much." They were more carefree or careless; they always sensed that they could relax more and minimize their worries.

One day I would not worry about anything and then I said a bad word. I would confess myself easier out of this situation or I needed to find a way to confront Mariana and she needed to tell me exactly what happened and together we needed to figure out what to do.

Back to the conversation, I said, to my father again, "If Mariana doesn't want to tell the truth, I might mention her name on the reporter file. My father looked at me and said, "That is the moment you should be all ready to tell what you know and everything will be fine. You have to take the responsibility as if his words bring you hope."

16

When we were returning at dawn, the sun was already above the horizon. Francisco and I looked for a place on the island that was calmer, because the day was beautiful. We found a small kiosk in oriental style. The kiosk was inside the island enclosed by the forest. We rested after a wonderful night on the boat, and upon opening the door of the kiosk the sunlight shone on our faces.

How can I define my relationship without describing the conflicting noises and preferences. I could hear Francisco saying, "What on earth is wrong with your family?"

"It t is partly my cousin's fault," I said, "screaming as a wolf."

I couldn't tell him about a moment I ran into a tree. And I felt like I should go faraway because I didn't know exactly where we were. I wanted to run into the street with my poor head trembling. I didn't want to talk. In an attempt to run fast I failed and I hurt my foot pretty bad. Francisco felt sad and said he didn't want to follow me because he knew it would only make things worse.

He screamed my name. "Lara?" he said. "Sorry, are you ok?"

I said, "No, please help me; I hurt my knee."

"Sorry about my questions ... I don't know how to help you. Don't worry, Francisco! The confusion is already there!"

"Okay, let me help you." He held me by his side and I tried tensing and jumping with one leg. With the other one I couldn't step on the ground.

"Oh, Lara," he said in a soft voice. "I know you're dealing with this pain! Why the Frick you don't tell me the truth ... what made you think different?" Francisco started, stuck again with the same questions!

"I just wanted to relax. I said. "I wished to be here with you and listen. I did not want to talk about things that were not resolved yet! And some are already gone." That person does not exist anymore – It's not a possibility of any return."

Francisco had to be quiet for a minute and recognize himself as being overwhelmed with questions and annoyed.

"Well, what was I to think?"

He tried one more time, except mentioned my cousin.

I said, "Maybe you should ask someone from my family?"

He quacked and waved his head like a duck. And I laughed because of how he quacked. It was like Donald Duck.

And he said, "Maybe!"

17

I had no clue or maybe I didn't care to deal with reality so I began to simply take deep, ragged breaths. I wasn't ready to force myself into a calm position.

I said to Francisco, "Let's get the boat and return to the house."

He grew quiet and said, "Fine, give me a couple hours. I need to prepare the boat and put in things that we may need.

I said, "Sorry I can't help you and I felt wasted because I couldn't move faster.

"Oh, don't worry, Lara. I can do this quickly before it gets darker." Francisco added." "Or maybe we can stay one more night."

I said, "I have medicine if you need to release the pain in your foot."

He said, "I can take you closer to the waves; waves from the ocean can help us to relax."

I said, "Yes – my father likes to go to the beach because it helps relax his muscles and the ocean salt is a medicine. He's always saying that."

By the time Francisco got things done, it was a little late, so we decided to stay the night at the cabin. It was turning out to be one of those most interesting nights.

Francisco started to laugh because I noticed to my surprise, a book inside where there were pictures. We'd taken them a long ago at the carnival. Francisco with long hair combed very high, used a very tiny short one that was ripped and tight. It was funny!

I asked him if he would wear this kind of short hair again, and he said "Why?"

I said, "Because it took years to change and become a different person with different ways and vision and views to see the world today."

Fabricio looked down for a few moments and said, "I should wear it and never change. That time was my best time."

I said, "Sounds depressing."

He said, "I agree," handing me the picture, but not before he ripped it up.

"Oh shit," I said. I wasn't happy that he destroyed the photo, but for some reason I agreed, so I kept quiet. We knew that looking back could help us to keep going and grab for a better future. We left next morning though Fabricio tried to persuade me to stay one day more.

I said, "No, it is time to leave, plus I can't walk well and I can't do much in this house far away from the group." I continued, "Let's go because I could go to the doctor and check it out—make sure I didn't break anything. But the truth was, I was fine. I just didn't want to stay. I could no longer deal with so many questions. I did not want to focus on the past. I needed to be alone.

Finally, we parked the boat and with the two pieces of beautiful wood we rowed the boat. It was pretty again on that morning because the Sun was exactly between us. Francisco ended up rowing the oars fast. I noticed his eyes were caught just there in front of me. He had chocolate-colored eyes and his body was perfect. He was extremely good-looking, but I couldn't stay with him because ... I needed to find comfort and be able to trust him. But I recognized that he was a good man also. I couldn't blame him for what happened and I realized that it was not fair to him nor to myself.

Took us about three hours back to the place where we talked with the group. It seemed that this all took many days.. I remembered feeling relieved and a little safer back all together.

18

The day was approaching for us to leave. They all came back in love, Roberto and Paula had already set the date of their engagement, Ricardo and Carla were flirting. We arrived in Guaratuba days near the end of February after the carnival. The first thing we went to visit was our beautiful Living Moon beach. Even with sad memories of the place it seemed that it was our beach. After the carnival we all went back to college. Mariana returned to her house, and seemed very ready to start a new life and be together. She was out of drugs, but she still looked for freedom. We were able to deal with the death of my cousin without sheer disgust and a feeling of relief that he died.

The memories were sad but I don't feel sad about her too. Meeting my cousin was the worst thing that happened in my life. He always found ways to abuse me. . Later she said that my cousin had forced her to do the abortion."

I was often feeling afraid and numb, and sometimes confused about what happened to me. I was both mad and sad to tell my parents because they may make me feel guilty, ashamed, and embarrassed. My cousin always acted as if nothing ever happened.

I remembered the first time my cousin, was with us at the Living Moon beach. It was a very hot summer. I already felt like an adult with the desire to make all the decisions. My cousin came to talk to me and I yelled at him and said, "I hope you die...!"

He laughed and ran up on a rock to do cliff-jumping at his only favorite spot, but unfortunately there were rocks in the water below and he had an accident and became paralyzed, finally dying of leg cancer. I felt no guilt inside because I wished that he would die, no remorseful feelings. Years later, I told my aunt what he did to me and also to Mariana. I do not know if Mariana mentioned to my aunt that she was pregnant by him.

I knew she started using drugs, and more drugs had been taken as 'havens' for freedom.

Mariana stopped and stared at the class from

afar. She knew that she had not fully been cured from that addiction. She had been strong enough to overcome for a while without the help of clinics, but she knew that the time was too short to be able to totally forget. And she did not want to, despite seeing them apparently happy. But she was strong enough to walk away without communicating. We were worried.

The other day Mariana told me in the most graphic terms exactly what had happened to her—about everything, her feelings, her inner battles, the need to find someone who truly loved her.

After ten years, Mariana found her brother. When her parents and brother had the accident on the boat, apparently, Mariana's brother was taken by a couple who never returned him to the family. The police found Mariana's parents, but her brother's body was never found. They all thought they were dead and so her brother never was discovered. Years later he attained freedom and ran away, left the person who kidnaped him for ten years. He could not be away from the island. The couple had a weird code system around the house that could signal if he tried to escape.

The couple were doctors that wanted to do an experiment to increase the Native Indian population by increasing the number of pregnancies taking place on the colonies around the island. The children and teens were always in the basement when someone from the police or government was around. Thus, nothing ever was found. It was unsure how the boy was able to escape from the Island and communicate with Mariana.

He said, "Mariana, you may well have a lot of nieces and nephews at the Island... I am not sure how many."

But Mariana and her brother soon built their trust and the relationship became stronger. I was in shock with all the histories and sad moments that my friend experienced.

One day I was walking with Mariana and I asked about her brother, Marcelo, and how he escaped from the illegal village. She tried to remember but she became more and more angry about it.

I knew Marcelo, but I do not feel comfortable to talk about it with him. It seemed so personal, and he didn't want to talk either. Mariana said that sometimes he grew so mad and frustrated in the city. She said, "It seems that he finds it very difficult to function in society, and many times I found him very quiet, and disconnected from his family. I'm not sure why he gets so mad, and sometimes I get impatient with him."

I said to Mariana, "Maybe you will not like my opinion, but life for your brother at the village was not easier. There was no one to trust, and he was even unsure if his family was alive or dead."

"It wasn't easier for me here either," Mariana said. "I wish he was here at the time; I missed them all."

I said to Mariana, "Give your brother a chance to live without judgment and questions, He will open up to you soon. Give him a time for himself; what do you think?"

He said, "Yes, I have to do that or else I may never see him again.

But Mariana said that one day her brother talked about how the village functioned. The place looked like a hostel in the basement; it functioned with many operations, many machines. He saw many young girls pregnant, but no babies around. It seemed that the babies were sent away pretty quickly for illegal adoption or trafficking. Mariana said that her brother now was foreign to everything outside the basement. He was the one that kept moving stuff from place to place. As he grew up a worldly young man, tall and strong like our father, he soon started to have sex with older girls at the village where he said to me, "Later I saw them with a baby on their belly, but I never was able to ask any questions."

And he said, "I have to keep quiet and each time I had sex; I knew there would be someone else like me around."

Mariana said to me, "He has hope that one day he will find his children."

I said, "It feels like that would be a very tragic miracle."

Mariana said, "His mind is twisted. He's thinking like if he could get help from law enforcement he'd maybe see where those babies were sent."

So, I asked Mariana, "I thought the leaders, doctors from the village, wanted to increase their population?"

"Well, not exactly," Mariana explained to me. "They sold the infants only after days or a week."

I said, "That is so sad, and the mothers felt miserable, I imagine."

Mariana said, "I couldn't imagine how horrible it would be. I was with my parents on the day of the accident; who knows if I could be one of the girls growing up at the village and I would be one of the girls at the village giving them babies and never knowing to whom they sent my own baby. That is so Frick crazy." And, then she said, "Which was worse? To be there at the compound or be abused by Alfonso and be pregnant and lose a baby?"

"Both ways are very awful; as a human being you

didn't deserve either path." I took a breath, and I began running a little bit faster forward to this beautiful sight.

And I said, "Run quickly, Mariana, see this place up there that is so beautiful." I didn't remember seeing it before. It is a large and beautiful garden over which you could take a gondola ride go from one place to another. That is so lovely."

19

I was dreaming in my own way to live my life and understand the way up and down, but never to give up. Sometimes I'd throw away some thoughts and desires that always came and affected my routine. People think that time passes so fast. I constantly think that my time is passing so much faster. My nightmares are on the list along with my ship full of fantasies. This year I would cross space. I will follow the winds and win the speed of time. I continually wanted to follow the movements existing in every living particle belonging to the Greek world. I know that everything sounds crazy ... when I spent a few years on the island of Crete, I lived with the people on all sides. I counted stones along where I passed each day. I lived in the narrow hills so narrow that sometimes I couldn't even breathe. I plunged into the caves, and found myself in the silence of my dreams.

I was living inside a shell and attempting to breathe all the earthy air and make the universe penetrate my heart, my skin. And right in the center of Crete Island, I was living in my all-snow-colored castle, around only the green of nature and the blue of the sea enveloping the moon. I saw myself writing the last chapter of my life. I woke up nervous and scared.

I remembered many years in the past. I was feeling scared to open the front door of my house in Sao Paulo. I had suffered many days of bad dreams and could no longer accept that everything was fine or going to be fine. I lost my brother and felt that someone was created by God to take his place. It never came to mind that someone could betray her best friend, that as a family we call a brother.

Father said, "Alexandre, you are like a son to us. Never disrespect my family."

My brother's work time was at night. He worked for a company to create machines that produce electricity--he corrected errors. He was responsible for secret information about the company's policy. After my brother finished his work it was about three in the morning, but Thursday he said, "I will be home soon."

My father said, "Why, the company will close Friday for inspection." My brother had the respect of the company and that company allowed him to bring a pen drive to work at home. He sometimes had charts he brought home with him.

On a Thursday night my brother did come. I heard someone strike the door very hard. My room was not too far from the door. My parents awoke for the same reason.

Later my mother, said she was not feeling well, so, my father opened the door quickly and in a second everything in my house changed.

The police told us that my brother had been shot, and my father and mother were calm for second. They started to process what the officer said. I could hear my mother's voice extremely anguished. As she opened the door a little, I saw her body shaking. She asked the officer to tell her the truth. The officer was calm the whole time. In my house, everyone was in pain and very lost, the crushing sadness was reflected on every face.

My mother immediately asked what happened, and the officer said, "Your son ended up in this country house, a little bit far from the city. He apparently knocked on the door. This woman answered from inside and complained that his voice didn't come out loud, and she could not understand much. The one word that was clear was water, he asked for water, and the woman gave some to him, later we heard that she felt guilty." She felt like she should be wiser at the time, because usually experts don't give water to a dying person, especially when the person has been shot. We lay on the floor for many hours. My father followed the police in his car, and asked, "Who did that?"

The police said, "You don't know but the person who shot your son, was looking for something else. Someone dropped him outside the county, but we found his car very close to the lady where he asked for help."

How did my brother end up in this situation? He was an appreciated man and it seemed everyone loved him.

On Saturday morning two days later, we were at the cemetery burying my brother. I tried to talk to my parents, and pretended that we could make conversation. My parents could talk with no tears on their faces. Me too, but I loved my older brother, and he was cool...–very nice.

Alexandre, told my middle brother Lucas, "I'll meet your brother for a few hours before he leaves. We were at the bar, but he left earlier and that was a red flag, because before he left he did say he talked to my brother that day."

So, Alexandre didn't tell the truth; but he continued coming to my parents' house. One day my relatives heard that Alexandre had a great amount of jealousy and animosity toward my brother. I don't know what the issues were, but I have to believe that Alexandre had a lot to do with my brother's death.

A week after the funeral, on a Friday, I was to return from the farmer place, and I know no one was in the house. I was off work and school that week. I opened the gate, oh, no I remember, the gate was broken and on the ground. I went straight to open the door, but while I did so I saw someone quickly jump out the first window room, which was my brother's room. I was in shock; I couldn't handle the moment. It was the kind of moment when you're torn between running off to catch the guy, or running into the house to see if everything is okay. My brother, for obvious reasons, had something that someone was looking for, someone thought he needed whatever he had... I assumed it was his pen drive and safe code from his company, and I recognized the guy. It happened very fast but I saw Alexandre. I couldn't prove it, but God knows.

My family brainstormed many ways to figure how the perpetrator killed my brother and got away. Days passed and we became only more convicted that Alexandre but and the police didn't have enough documentation to suspect him guilty. He deserved to be in jail. Many dishonesties flew from Alexandre's mouth leaving great concern about his behavior

My brother's friend raised many questions about Alexandre's behavior. One of his friends said, "Alexandre has been struggling with money, and he wanted to buy stuff and drive to Paraguay, as if just maybe he wanted to become a member of the mafia, that sell illegal products without documentation." So, to make sense, he wanted to steal my brother's pen drive with information on how to build the electrical tanks. It sounded like he wanted to sell the information.

I didn't want to see him anymore, once I really wanted to confront and beat him, but I couldn't physically nor emotionally. But I really wanted to do something to make him suffer. I said to my mother, "My change of decision for not riding someone to beating him to death is because I care for the family, and later someone will discover that we did that. When I heard that Alexandre could move to Paraguay, I learned of an address change. And he was running from one place to another. I told one of his friends that I didn't care."

The days continued to be very sad for all of us. We each sat at the table quietly and the less questions we asked, the better it was for everyone. I understood the silence, but I never forgot my brother's last days with us I felt that I could have done more, but lack of experience in dealing with the situation froze me in place, wondering why this happened to him.

I told myself I needed to continue to live my life. My brother would never be back anymore. And I couldn't stay at my parents' house anymore, first because I had to return to work, and second, I needed to finish my last semester. I had asked if they would ever consider moving out to peace and comfort outside of Sao Paulo? I told them, "Let me know if I can do anything to help."

I was already making good money at my work, and I had a lot saved. When, my godmother died she left more than enough money for me to pay my school tuition, so I didn't have to ask to use my parents' money. I had enough for them to rent a nice place in another city, without selling the present house and everything else. I saw them disillusioned with everything and living at the same house was making the feeling worse. I talked to my aunts that lived in another city by Helo Horizonte, to invite them to stay for a few months.

The months that my parents spent in my aunt's house, with my mother's sister--that time with them helped her work through a lot of issues between her and the whole family. My mother left home at a young age, and moved with my father and the whole family, and the whole community knew what happened. Again, she said, "I prayed for the next generation. I had to be mindful about my family cycle, and unhappy things that we were carrying from generation to generation. And I was trying to break the family cycle. I was building flexibility while I thought about our family history. I began feeling closer to my ancestry in a way. I also started to understand that some things don't belong to me.

Those stories arrived in my life unbidden. I was looking for answers and learning to place boundaries on my cravings. I was walking down my parent's path without controlling my thoughts, the best way to get to know yourself... At least I thought I was on the right path. I was maddened by all the fake letters that were sent to my great -great, and the struggles to control many lives among my relatives. I got to know how I was here and growing up with an understanding that genetic behaviors are transmissible through our good old DNA. Depression had disconnected and struck down some relatives that lived years without letting their salience be their guidance along an intimidating way. Not only behaviors bring you down, but sad feelings surrounding some member of my family that some don't like to deal with. Growing up, most of the time we heard that depression is a behavior of a person who did not want to do their fair share, and then, people from outside making a judgment. Outsiders would declare, "They want a break from responsibility, they don't want to do nothing…"

My mother didn't let the bad feelings control her. As soon as she noticed, she tried to change and force herself back to normal as soon as possible, and also my father could not allow her to lie on the bed just doing nothing.

My mother, came from a hard-working family, finished college and learned a way to keep herself alive and in good health. She had to keep everything under control at the house, like the assumption that none of her kids made an error, a mistake that others might have made.

My grandmother had a heart condition that she never told us about, and when my brother died, her heartbeat became weaker and more erratic and I noticed significant signs of depression.

Being an adult person, I had responsibility and compassion to help her, and being the older sister, I had to remind her to save her life, no matter how difficult it became.

When I was born, I eventually learned that my mother had a personal problem that never was made clear, but she survived. Somehow the miracle and enjoyment of life brought her a peace. My two younger sisters and my two brothers, then me. Being with a lot of people in the house brought more work and responsibility, but also helped alleviate her tension, and there were less extreme mood changes.

One day I saw her trying to save a baby bird and was talking to the bird. I thought this was so beautiful. She brought the baby bird inside the house to protect him from the weather and from predators. She could leave the bird there for the bird's mother to take care, but it was raining heavily with strong wind and the bird nest fell on the floor. My mother said, "I was afraid that the mother wouldn't come back right away. So, I hope I did the right thing..."

I said to her, "Of course, Mother and I kissed her." My mother always found a way to bring pets to the house. One day, she brought a dog, a cat, and a pig on the same day... My father, said, "No, no," and just kept the dog. She didn't like it, but, after all, there was no space.

This was not the life that I was looking for. I was scared and for sure this was not my reality.

By the age of six I was very small yet already dreamed of having a different life. Things suddenly felt different but I was surrounded with orders difficult to follow sometimes. I had to learn fast from my friends, and my family needed to see that I was adjusted to this new school. Within a few months I turned seven. I needed to be all ready for the first grade. So, I needed to be a good girl.

School started at the end of Carnaval in Brazil. I was shy and felt lonely sometimes. A new girl named Marcia joined my class, and soon we became friends. Her parents acquired a temporary residence permit to move to Brazil. Her father was from Japan and her mother was from Taiwan. Both worked for an army so they could move around the Globo.

Her mother was a great-granddaughter from a military family who served in 1941 as the operator of Barbarossa troops. But Marcia's mother worked as a nurse at the base and became involved in a common nuclear cooperation with Brazil. Also, keep in mind that they were able to establish better control of Brazil's interest in the Amazon. The competition between countries seemed to always include the Amazon. And my greatest interest was located along the Brazilian borders, which had beautiful views and a lot of medicines. They wanted to provide and show goals that would effectively control the border. But I knew that the end would not be pretty. So, when Marcia's parents finished the project and increased the number of posts and army to the border that was the end of their lives and Marcia was able to attend only nine months in my school; I was shocked and very sad. Every day I cried and cried and I could not understand why she was gone.

My birthday was supposed to be my special day; I was gifted with this beautiful doll, the one I could walk with every place I went, and I could talk with her any time, and I was so happy that I could lay my doll in bed. She could close her eyes, and when I picked her up, she could open her eyes. I named her Marcia, and she became my little best friend. One of my favorite things was singing her to sleep at night.

One morning, I went with my mother to visit the neighbor who lived a block away. Our neighbor wanted to donate a puppy. The dog was so special she was named Rosa, a good breed "Fila" (Rosa, pronounced in Portuguese 'Flor'). She gave birth to eight puppies! very cute--adorable, five female puppies and three males. I remember every time I reached the neighbor's house, I always asked, "Where is your dog?" She always responded "my baby Rosa" is sleeping or doing something else.

So, I went to take my doll to show to our neighbor, but Marcia was sleeping. Then I said to my mother, "I won't take Marcia with me to the neighbor," and my mother asked, "Who?"

I said, "My doll. I miss seeing her face Anyway I didn't bring her today.

On the way back I was talking to my mother about my little friend, and she asked me, "What is the name again?"

"Marcia, she is my new friend."

I said, "And this is my doll called Marcia."

She said, "The girl from your school is named Marcia, is that right? She is a lucky girl; you just got a new doll and named her Marcia."

I said, "Yes, I wish I could tell her." We were the same age. She was a spoiled girl who had lots of dolls and clothes. But she was very nice to me and with everyone in class.

I arrived at home and I went straight to my room. I screamed so loud, that everyone came to see what happened. My doll had a hole in each eye. It was so scary. Who did that? This exact doll was my best friend. Anyone who looked could see that Marcia was not a simple cheap doll. It was the only toy I had that I took care of like a real baby. That was so special and unique. But who did that?" I was yelling and asking many times. "Who did that?"

So many people in the house, children and relatives were at our home that day. No one saw the one who committed the crime. Everyone was quiet. Seemed that no one saw what happened.

A few days later I heard my older brother playing with my blind doll. He had made a fake eye. He glued a very tiny white ball and colored it and drew an eye on each side. I asked, "Where did you get that thing?"

He said, "I bought glue, ball and papers."

"What are you thinking? You looked scared? "You didn't realize dolls cannot die?"

I realized that Marcia was not the same, but I could still play with her. Each day I felt challenged to take care of Marcia. I found myself down for trying to help Marcia sleep. The truth was that the doll couldn't close her eyes anymore. The way my brother reconstructed her, the eyes could move. But I still wanted to know who did the horrible thing of gouging Marcia's eyes out. I tried doing my normal activities and keeping my doll closer to me. I used to go to my room and talk to Marcia, my little friend, so whenever I was in the room, I would be talking to her, but I could see her strangely painted eyes. It was not real anymore. At first, I had been happy it gave me a joy; but that did not last long. Soon, I became scared of the doll. I did not know how to talk with her anymore.

One afternoon I came home from school and rushed into the room as usual to see Marcia. I froze. I went back to the living room and I asked my mother to take the doll out of my room. She said, "Are you sure?"

I said, yes!

I could not see my mother moving Marcia from my room. My eyes would not meet her fake eyes. What was I doing?

A few days afterward, my mom talked about the puppies, and then she asked, "Lara, you want to see the puppies again?"

She knew that I needed to get over Marcia, and a puppy would be good at this time. And I said "Yes," remembering being so excited about seeing them.

When we got to Nara, the neighbor's house, all the puppies were so cute. Already a week older, all the puppies lay beside Rose, the mother. The puppies were still very small. I asked, "Nara, did you name the puppies?"

She said, "Yes, let me see if I can remember

the names. She started by saying the names of the males: Lucas, Lucas had a big spot on his back, Fula, was very fast and all black, she named the last puppy boy, Fast. And I asked," How about the girls?"

Then she got confused a little but she was able to remember them all. All the puppy's females seemed smaller, but the cutest, the first one who saw me had a tail with some spots and otherwise all white, the other three were brown and their ears had some white spots, and the last one was mixed white and brown and plus, she had small black spots all over her body, Nara named her "Adora" because Joana loves Amora. "Amora" is a fruit in Brazil—very delicious, like "Blackberry" her tiny black spots.

Then I asked my mom, "Can I have one of the puppies? Now, today?"

Before she asked Nara, she told me, "No, because the puppies need to stay with their mom until they get strong, and they need to be able to walk, run, and eat solid food. So, she said, "I need to wait at least eight weeks."

And I said, "The puppies will be about two months?"

"Yes," Nara responded.

I checked the calendar every day, and I said to my mom "Only six days left!"

Finally, I got Adora. I loved my new puppy, I usually called her "Adora, "Eu adoro voce, "This means in Portuguese: "Adora, "I love you."

Of course, we had many episodes of number one and number two in the house. In a few days Adora learned to do her pee and poop.

But I was a little disenchanted with Marcia, my doll. I didn't enjoy playing with her anymore. I realized that I was going to give away Marcia. I had to tell my mom. I felt quite proud of myself regarding my decision.

I spent the day around Marcia most of the time. That evening, I sat very close to Adora, and had a real play time. She jumped, ran around, and barked looking so happy.

After playing for a minute or so. I told my mom, "Carefully take Marcia from my room."

I was very sad, and for a minute I changed my mind and asked my mother to leave Marcia in my room. I guessed I was not quite ready to say good-bye to Marcia. I saw that all my feelings were there and I had done right. The decision helped me that day.

Every day I was feeling better and better about missing my friend Marcia, until my grandmother passed away with an infection while receiving treatment for a kidney problem in the hospital. We couldn't believe. It was too much, the whole family was depressed at once, everyone was down. I was so miserable, very sad, that I could not say an appropriate good-bye to my grandmother, and I was so mad too. I remember my body was sore and my attitudes at the beginning made me want to be away from everybody. I didn't want to talk.

I tried so many times and I could not give away Marcia, my doll. Now I carried much lonelier feelings, I needed her to talk. I remember, my father came and he spoke to me. "Are you okay?"

We didn't talk too much. My father used to work a lot and travel a lot too. But now, I needed to communicate more with him. He tried to bring a sense of the familiar after my grandmother passed way. To me I was a little bit late because I always was shy and quiet, as my personality let me guide my intelligence in relation to what I wanted.

After a year of missing my grandmother, my mother asked me if, "I was ready to say goodbye to Marcia and to my grandmother. I said, "yes!"

My father said, "We are going to move to another city and it's time to say goodbye to the old things, but never forget the good memories. This "moving thing," seemed a new life—a time to catch new opportunities. I asked my father, "It's true that we won't come back here anymore?"

He said, "Yes," (but he lied). We moved to Santa Catarina for two years, then we came back. The work he was doing at Santa Catarina didn't appeal the way it was expected to. So, to provide a better quality of life for all of us, he needed to return to Sao Paulo. I was kind of happy at Santa Catarina. I started a new school where all the kids seemed nice, and I tried to make as many friends as I could. At the beginning I thought it would take me awhile to adjust at school and make a new real friend. I was wrong.

My mom was always with me as a real person, not a doll. When my mum had to fight against her family about moving out with my father, she had to live by herself and figured out how to take care of herself. It was difficult since they took many freedoms without prior communication with the family

Marcia, my doll, my little friend. I never saw her again. The connection with my doll: "I think it was crazy. That she/it, the truth was my doll. She helped me at a time I was lonely inside, to break the silence, there was Marcia, letting me talk without interruption. And could there have been a better way to teach myself?

CARRIAGE OF MY DREAMS

20

Searching for my reality, I was seeing myself again on a road with dreams. And at dawn, the drizzle that fell softly, moistened the earth, softened my heart. I stood at the window, hoping that everything was nothing more than a feat of that creature, because I didn't even want to remember the shape or color.

I did wish I could see what was the matter. It passes so fast, snatching and killing my air--flashing lightning bolts between thunders. I would always watch it pass by, and then a carriage covered all over with sheets of rain and lace tape passed by.

It was a beautiful carriage; I was loving something that I never knew existed, but it was always a mystery. And I was quite frightened. The beautiful carriage only passed at ten o'clock and I could not see anyone inside it. Every day at this same hour, I climbed down from the window. The window was very high, and I had to climb onto a stool to be able to see it. I was always too short to see the carriage disappear over the horizon. At this time, I was so small that I looked like I was ten years old, but I was actually older than that. I was thin, with short hair, but in compensation I had a pair of eyes as big as marbles. I always imagined that God gave me those eyes so I could see all the things that I wanted to see, even if things were far beyond my horizon.

Alone, I spent days and days looking at that carriage passing. After a long time, I decided to call the boys, Renato and Rafael, my neighbors. We spent many hours playing in the shed that was in the backyard of my house. The shed was quite large, there was everything you could think of, from old machines, a bicycle and even a rusting car. But I wanted Rafael's father to help fix my bike. I wanted it to fly. The bike was beautiful, but was not really mine and strangely it didn't fly. I was sad because my dreams were passing and I could not catch them. I knew I could not reach that beautiful carriage like a satin rose that opened at dawn and closed in the twilight of the day. I spent hours and hours thinking that the carriage was just missing me, dressed in pink lace and blue ribbons, flying in space with my dreams.

The years passed, the carriage disappeared, leaving a longing for the dawn, the drizzle, and even a huge longing for my hungry heart to no longer dream of my sense of living with or without a satin carriage that appeared with the moon and disappeared in daylight's thin air. Until I realized, looking in the mirror years later, I saw that it was me in the carriage. So, I played with myself inside my eyes. I was always dreaming things that were impossible to reach. Again I was looking into my image.

21

The next day, at the same time as waiting for the carriage, my eyes were glued on the sky I had awaited for days and days at the base of the window without a screen and very dirty with birds' poop, alongside of dogs' and cats' poop. I cleaned up as much as I could. My brothers never cleaned up those things and thought it was great fun that those birds and animals always went to my window – not one time did anyone arrive to help me or ask me if I needed help – and one day I set out a box to pick one of the birds. I was introducing myself to him, calling him Blue because amazingly it was a real blue bird. Honestly, I heard so many meanings about blue birds, my parents both were very superstitious, saying the bluebird is a symbol of joy and hope. And my mother insisted good news would arrive – I was very happy because I hoped one day to see inside the carriage. Always I tried to get the bird and failed every time. I imagined if I caught the bird what magical things might happen.

Then came my father with his superstition to introduce his belief about the blue bird that supposedly represents a connection between the living and the dead. I thought, how am I going to deal with these two telling me about my foolish process and hope to make this blue bird a pet? It was really hard to get him. This kind of birds were smart and fast and I tried to use my imagination. Reading about them, I got one definition from the Bible "...The bluebird meaning in the Bible is that these birds are angels in disguise. They act as messengers from the realm of God, sent by our guardian angels to deliver an important message to people on Earth." Reading this meaning I grew very excited, interested and a little afraid to know what is the real message that the blue bird around my window wanted to tell me. There was only one way to find out—I must be patient. I laughed for a few minutes at the thought that a road runner like me could be patient. I arranged the box to try again to catch the birth.

I had somewhat dreamed but was also negligent in my actions, distracted by many people telling me what to do and unfortunately getting away without explanation. But it was time to go back to my real life: Today people still talk and make judgments against things they know little about. They spoil the reality and cover the existence of sin which makes them feel free for a moment. My mind grew extremely from the opposite direction, that I tried to be strong and smooth at the same time.

I dreamed about all the reality and fact around me. My job, people around me, whom I respected and I observed I kept with me. They illustrated to me the correct way to speak and behave. My way of life sometimes scared me; they were manners and attitudes that I attributed to many past generations.

While not being considered a vague person, sometimes I don't see how I can trust my past generation when I can't even take purely a way to explain how they were allowed to participate in a comfortable conversation, and sit down in a relaxed way to talk about basic self-respect. I could keep my eyes open for too long when I declared my dream to the world and fearfully waited for what their responses would be.

Again, I was looking into my image, coming back to my reality, "I'm a bad person, I made mistakes, and I'm going to die." I'm living, and I am dreaming, and I should learn that whenever we make mistakes it exposes us as different persons. We can be very alike but should not take that as license to be stupid.

I had a lot of dreams in my carriage; it seemed that I had to carry this big package that was heavy. And I had been traveling inside myself, and hoping that I would deliver some of these dreams in different places. I should look for a place that I dreamed of one day; this dream was very close to me.

When I was growing up, I was told that, if I kept driving my car recklessly, I would end up doing something wrong. And, I ended up doing things unwisely. When Rafael's father fixed it, I would be feeling a sense of reality, but I said to Jothan, Rafael's father, "This bike will fly and then I will catch dreams." And I added, "My carriage too?"

He said, "You need to pass by somewhat slowly, because dreams sometimes cross your life very quickly and you let them go, missing the meaning somehow."

Today, looking at my carriage, it seemed that some dreams died out. I remembered my mum saying, "Dreams give you the impression that your search for enjoyment will unceasingly be fulfilled." Because she said, "The dreams coming with your thoughts you believe, my daughter. You won't be able to catch all your dreams, but the ones that you do reach, you must always be thankful for. They are all from God."

I remember I planned to move out from my parents' house at age nineteen, and it was a big deal to my parents. In my culture, we moved out only after marriage or when attending college outside, but sometimes it's not an option, especially for the girls. I took the first step to move out, even before finishing college. I was home but figured that was my time to move out. I decided to apply for jobs outside my city, having been fired from my previous Lab because I broke the code. I did not regret telling what the Lab was doing. I remembered I had to write a report giving details of everything I saw and knew.

I was looking for a simple place to rent, my main goal was getting a place closer to my work so I could walk to my work every day; that was my plan.

When I decided to move from my small community in Sao Paulo, my plan was disrupted because my application indicated that I failed one of the tests. So, I was very disappointed. And when I called to get more information, I had a big surprise. Instead of having failed I had good news to keep me alive to my next position at work. The lady that placed my phone call said, "You didn't fail, it was showing that there was missing information and one test that you were supposed to take, although I was well aware that I did everything that I was supposed to do. And I thought, "I'm not crazy after all."

The human resources at the Lab set up a new date for me to do the test and the final interview. I was already over-vehement all those months waiting for the move out to start a new life. And, of course on the approval of my family. And, of course, I had an unpleasant talk with my brother, James. In his view it was never a good idea to move out alone and leave behind your family. I thought he wanted to be in control and see things revolve around him. But, he said "Why do you need to range up so far without your friends and find a job so far. Stay closer, you can have my car and finish your college."

"No, thank you," I said, and mentioned I needed to get this new job because the end result would be a very important position, and I may also have a very nice place to live much closer, so I needed to get this opportunity, I thought. I had no desire to live anymore in the big city.

His eyebrows writhed downward like two un-happy caterpillars, but then his lips moved upward in a faint smile and he said, "Good luck."

"I was afraid that my parents would make a big deal, and I was completely right.

"Lara Alberene!" When my father wanted to talk in a stern way, he called my entire name. And, then I knew that things were troubled in paradise!" He said, "Look for all your baggage," and then I felt a little embarrassed because I remembered Alfonso, and I felt a few tears roll down my cheek.

But he did mention about my cousin, because he did not even know what happened. Was it me my thoughts and whatnot, the word "embarrassed" brought me a feeling of concern and tragic thoughts that I did not want to deal with. But sometime I wanted to get to the state of a sense of reality—to lift up my soul over the sad, bitter things and see the possible beauty of a new life, a new thing.

I needed to tell my mother first about Alfonso. I felt an unrefusable compulsion to tell my father because inside me I knew that against my will I made a huge mistake as a much younger girl.

Well, I would be twenty, and I might need some help, and my parents needed to know what I had passed through all these years.

I had absolutely no idea how my parents would take this sad secret. I remembered telling my mother first. I figured she would scream out how I could keep such a violation of my innocence secret for so many years (over ten). She first cried, put her hand over her face, and then she hugged me very strongly.

I think at the moment she felt heartbroken for not knowing and for not protecting her daughter from my monster cousin, Alfonso.

"I had no idea exactly how deep was her grief

because she only repeated sorry over and over multiplied times. I remembered, it took my whole summer dealing with the explanation with my father while keeping strong and for some time he wanted to blame my mother for telling my cousin to go outside in the yard with me. I remembered my father's eyes definitely stared into my eyes and said, "Sorry, it never was totally our fault."

At this moment I recognized a change in my parent's relationship with me. It was also a beginning of a new relationship with both of them. The loss of understanding as to why my cousin did it. It again, was once a situation of shame that was never brought to a meaningful settling of grief. Simultaneously, was there an unspeakable rage around my great-great father for basically raping my great-great grandmother, Joana. And, again, that is a profanity to bring to a family cycle.

Frustratingly, I would have to go and find my space at my place without saying anything. I could go far away and forget everything. I thought I was supposed to keep this memory to myself and I could protect me from him and everyone else. I was so wrong.

I was emotionally addicted to my own thoughts; I had already talked to Mariana in an effort to forget all this. It was a real but contrasting feeling between the two of us when we talked about the same person in the past.

The shades of anger just showed up in Mariana's face all the time. Every time Mariana went to sleep, every day in the morning and after school, the memories came that she couldn't handle.

My true feeling was there in the darkness and I couldn't prevent myself from being irritated and always I missed the night. Instead of sleep, my thoughts didn't allow me to relax. I had a monstrous time falling asleep.

After I finally was able to talk for the first time with my parents, at the time I felt my chest lighten, and I noticed that I felt stronger. I remembered my mother, being hidden in her shame, even though she hugged me all the time. Actually, I never had a clue that she would feel this way, blaming herself all the time. My mother is very protective; she likes to know everything that is going on around us. At our young age she was always there to participate in events that my brothers and I participated in at school or another activity, soccer or any musical performance—even watching us play bets or a dodgeball game. It seemed that she wanted to be there and see all that was going on. AT the time I was always filled with love and a sense of protection, and it was wonderful .

I was safe and happy, and slowly I was moving, doing activities. There was a moment that I see my aunt there at the activities to bring her little daughter, and I remember hoping Alfonso didn't abuse his little sister. I almost punched his face. I started playing but inside me I really wanted to tell my mother and her sister-law, my aunt. Inside me was this breaking heart but I didn't know how to disperse these feelings. I hoping that someone would ask something and somehow I could tell the truth about Alfonso. And, every time I had a change of heart. I wasn't sure if someone would believe in me and also in Mariana.

Still, no one answered and of course no communication occurred between us about Alfonso. Every time after any activities or end of class, I went straight to my mother's car along with him. Once again, I thought that it would be just easier to delete all the memories. The sad part was that I wouldn't let him come closer to me, but Alfonso pushed me and tracked me again and again, with supposedly no worries, no given importance.

This happened before I had to tell my mother that I did not want to go to my aunt's house anymore. I said to my mother, "Those boys over at my aunt's house, they are stupid. They play too rough and Alfonso's cousin is very mean.

And she said, "You don't have to go anymore, and the next trip I will take you with me."

That moment I felt safe and I did not have anything to do with them anymore. I looked up at my mother and I hugged her and she seemed mystified at my extreme gratefulness. She asked me, "Is everything okay?"

I said, "Yes," and again, knew I should actually tell her the truth."

A few weeks passed, and I had the chance to confront Alfonso and his parents at his house. It was a birthday party for Alfonso's little sister. My young cousin was now turning seven years old. The whole family was invited, but my older sister wouldn't come; she was visiting my grandmother. We came early to the birthday party, because my mother was supposed to make a salad. This was the special salad that my mom loved to make, and everyone savored it. It was nice to be there with

My parents and more relatives and guests. The only ogre was Alfonso

I decided to not stay closer to the kids because he constantly slunk around the kids. Instead of staying with them, I enjoyed some time around my mother and her friends and remained with them the whole time.

I felt safe, and I took time to talk to my little cousin, Sofia. She is adorable, and owned a lot of toys and dolls. It made me remember my doll, Marcia. I grabbed a favorite doll of hers, but didn't know anything until she said, "Oh! That is my baby doll; she is sleeping but you can hold her if you are gentle."

Oh! Sorry Sofia, I will be very careful and talk soft." She ran outside to play with her friends from school.

I remember I asked my mother to buy a doll for Sofia as a gift. But she'd bought a bike for her because her mother said to my mother, "That Sofia already has so many toys and dolls."

At the party I ate cake that my mother baked, and I had two cups of apple juice, made fresh from my aunt's apple trees, and a popsicle. I walked around a little, following some kids. At one point, I smiled as the father tried to pop the balloons, it was comical. And finally he grew tired and pushed out a chair to relax for a minute.

I remembered my aunt asked my Cousin Alfonso, to come into the house. I noticed that he was running and playing hard with a small kid. It seemed he had a mental problem. He elected to stay in the kitchen and help his father a little by putting ice in the cooler and pick some dirty cups off the floor. I quietly asked my mother to fill my cup with apple juice. I was now outside while he was inside the house. I waited until he had done his task.

I was by the fence inside. It had a big post, and I was there leaning against it. To my surprise my aunt came behind me and said,

"Why you don't play with the other kids?" and then she said, "I know you know some teenagers. And they are beautiful and smart."

I glanced around nervously, and for a minute I wanted to tell my aunt that her son, Alfonso is a really bad boy, and he would surely die soon, because he was a monster." But I couldn't and I also hadn't seen my aunt so happy until this moment. Since my grandmother died she'd become so depressed. At the funeral she passed out and she missed the whole memorial service.

In reality, I glanced down and then turned my face away. I only hugged her, and she left with a big smile.

Courage is what it takes to tell, but I just couldn't uncover Alfonso's secret. I lived in a succession of years, days, hours and minutes that involved my

soul, my heart, which now brings me to the notion of the present, the memories of the past, and the strong imagination regarding a very close and real future.

In these times I made myself first graceful, and started counting my days. From that moment I began to share myself with people who care about me.

The day that I bound my personality in a new positive emotion, I began growing stronger, deciding I must forget the dark past.

I remembered telling Francisco, "My brain sometimes works twice as hard and together it brings me a formula of forgiveness. Together my pain fits perfectly in my mind as if it were a missing long-forgotten living cell.

My memories about my early childhood brought me longings for a different story, tears fell, but I tried to always smile a little through the tears. I knew that I had a great example at my home with great dynamism.

I speak of these two tales of my carriage where I always was looking for Francisco; although these hard words are truth, I have sought to convey my gratitude to a single person in particular: "God," who so generously covers me with faith and makes me feel a true pure passion as a person. I said to Francisco, "I confess to you that the passion I'm feeling for you is real. It is a common life in which we were born at the same time."

Francisco said to me, "You were looking, searching for your identification and in time, you found it straightforwardly. From your origin emerged a silence that understood the mystery of beating hearts and eternal romance."

The Blue Moon was full of unforgettable adventures that reunited their birthrights. It required many actions with a drastic suspension from reality. These were moments of strong tension in the plot of a broken romance in sync with a discovery of consequent responsibilities. Yet every moment seemed to pass at a fast pace.

I said to Francisco, "Those facts both fascinate and can also hurt you!"

ETERNAL RETURN

22

Friday was supposed to be a long holyday. I was at my Aunt Teresa's house. At the time, she was living outside Sao Paulo city. When I arrived to stay with her for the weekend, my middle brother, James, was there. I didn't know that my middle brother had made a plan to visit my aunt.

Actually, she was not my real aunt by blood. She was adopted from my grandparents when she was five years old. So, she became part of the family as she is more than an aunt. She was my favorite one. She always took care of me, and always made my favorite fries, which she just cut in four chunks and fried. Just the way I loved, everything was prepared for me before I even reached her house. She was always saying, "Your room is already there; one day you will stay there many days."

The truth behind that visit from my brother

was because he'd become interested in our cousin, Catarina, but not through bloodlines. My brother and his girlfriend met Mariana at the bar—actually, outside of the bar, and Mariana was with her influential group, though at the time she was out of balance. She was wild with no idea that Mariana could go this far outside Sao Paula to hang out with her group.

Anyway, at dinner time at my aunt's, we were all together: my uncle, my two cousins and my cousin Catarina, and myself. Again, my aunt made my favorite crisp French fries, delicious. And they all were saying that my aunt spoiled me. I, of course, knew, but I said, "I imagine she already had this prepared for everyone."

During dinner, my brother mentioned about my friend. He said, "I saw your friend last night at the bar."

And, I said, "Which friend?"

He was very polite and said, "It's your friend, her parents died on accident. I think her name is Mariana?"

"Oh, yes, you'd seen her at the house before not very long ago?"

He said, "Yes" and we kind of started a little discussion at the dinner table at my aunt's house. At the time I didn't understand all the questions.

Then, someone at the table said, "I believe it was one of my cousins, who brought memories about my birthday present."

"I don't think it's funny; of course it was about my doll, Marcia."

With my thoughts I was far away from the table for a Segundo. "What happened with Mariana, my brother, and Catarina last night," I remarked I have not been talking with her for a few days." And then, I said, Maybe we should not talk about dear Mariana unless she is here to defend herself, am I not correct?"

My aunt and the rest at the table, then avoided talking about the past, and especially about Mariana." So after we quickly changed the subject, we discussed the future: my aunt and uncle wanted to buy a farm closer to this very special place where a Brazilian film was produced called "Pica Pau Amarelo."

But I really wanted to know the truth and I was imagining what happened on that night, which made my brother look at me as if very disappointed.

Next day in the morning I left, and in the lateness of the day, I called Mariana. We talked as usual, we laughed together for a bit because, she was telling me that her grandmother bought a wireless phone, and told Mariana, that she needed to hang up because she needed pick up something. And she completely forgot that she could take the phone and walk or drive down the street with it." During the conversation, I asked her "Did you see my brother and my cousin last Friday?"

For a minute she didn't recall, but she quickly remembered a couple was staring at her. "I remember," she said. "He looked familiar and I was wondering who the guy was?" Later her memory became clearer.

And then she said, "That is James, your brother."

And I said, "Yes," he asked me questions about you, and what you were doing in front of the bar with a stranger.

First, it was not a stranger, guys; they were my friend's brothers. They wanted me to drive them back and my brother was bothering me because they were drunk and I didn't want them to drive, but also, I didn't want to stay there any longer. So, we had a little fight. It was dark–around 1:00 am. Maybe your brother had noticed that I was drunk and into drugs again, with a bad guy. So, he had different reactions." She said, "That is disgusting that people always assume things, and forget to offer help."

I apologized to her and I said, "Forget that you ever saw my brother. He is like a turkey that always smells of bad things, even if there are none.

One day I had nothing to do so I stopped at my older sister's home Rose asked me to stay for afternoon coffee. I said "Yes, it's a good idea. I need to stay up late anyway to finish some work for tomorrow. But I regret to say; I can't stay more than a couple sips of the coffee.

James arrived very anxious and worried about his job. Anyway, I said to him, "This will get better."

And, he said, very angrily, "Like your best friend?" And he tried to be in control of the situation, and wanted me to break my relationship with Mariana, because he thought she was "not a good girl." I stopped and spoke softly, "Exactly who are you to tell me what to do? I live my life the way I want and I choose my friends, and my Mariana, will continue be my best friend."

He got furious and slapped my face so hard it left a scarlet handprint that didn't get better for two or three days. I left my sister's house without saying anything.

Of course, it took a while for him to apologize. Unsuccessful, he always wanted to be the man of the house, just like my great-great father. As my father said once, "I did like to spend time with my great grandfather because he always wanted to intimidate the women and I didn't like the way he talked." My brother could be a good guy, but he also could be stupid when he thought or imagined that he was all-knowing.

For a month I was quiet; I didn't talk to my brother. The family got mad with James, considering his actions very inappropriate and devoid of respect.

When he started a conversation, I just responded to him in a few words, only as much as were necessary. And, finally, he said, "I am sorry." It seemed hard for my brother to allow himself to both admit regret and show kindness.

"Well," I said, "there is always a return from the point you think that someone is wrongfully hurt." When I got into deep conflict with my parents, it seemed that everything came to a head exactly the same, plainly, but it always captured my fear, and everything gradually changed. It was like my parents to end up completely separated by views, but similarly alike regarding the absolute two laws of Nature that engage with the law of truth and how they can understand the philosophy of the crazy nature inside human beings. It would be like creating a new universe, an evolution of eternal return—an encounter with new planets on a single stage.

That's me trying to tell my friends how they found the eternal return through the law of conquest...

For some moments they accused me of pushing my cousin. I had a very difficult time proving my innocence. It was very complicated because of my aunt and I liked her very much. I think I was a person who dreamed too much... in one of the dreams I was strolling on an island. I even remember the name of the island, Beautiful Island. I was there for a long time before you were born.

It was the first time I felt the urge to let my thinking take shape, and to show the reasons... I cried with emotion but I was relieved. The day had come to leave. There were more people with me, and we packed everything up and I left. I did not want to stay around these people anymore. Not far away, the gas ran out, but I continued to walk. I began to realize that I was lost and, to top it off, it began to rain that horrible icy drizzle.

When I arrived at a small unknown and lonely house I fell asleep. At dawn, the sun appeared. Frightened, I asked, "What place is this?" It was very quiet. I had no answer. I was sad. It wasn't mine on that corner, it wasn't me who lived in this place, but I confess the place was beautiful. There were huge trees that were born in front of the sea as if protecting something.

I came to be madly in love with the place. The sea, the little house, the coconut trees, the sands were so fine-everything was as beautiful as a dream — I thought, here I could be happy until death. Suddenly, it gave me a great fear to imagine there is no death, only a fear of death. What a silly thing; I woke up again!

I began to worry about giving a name to this new island through which I might find a passage in my world that I could select for the future. The future that we did not know, yet future that only GOD knows I could make plans and fight for my destiny no matter how challenging, thrilling or intimidating life is around me.

I saw that the time was passing fast and I kept up with the time. I was even able to advance the time periodically by doing things faster…. In the enchantment of the island I enveloped myself as if bewitched by the small bungalow. I kept looking at this beauty which revived my life. That made me generate another life, another me.

The silence, the peace, provided evidence that this house had been made for me--the charm, the mystery, made me remain for many years on that island where I was perched on the only living islet.

And how was I to survive? It was a miracle, and in it you were borne through time, emotions, tears and longing...

Today I call myself from time to time in short stories and poetry, innocently without realizing one day I wanted to overflow in the darkness of the civilization of sin I made mistakes that would cause me to grow with fear. Growing in fear hurt me, but I kept hiding my feelings... my pain. I just told myself, "No, I am not fine." for I still believed that I never should show emotion when I can figure exactly how to proceed and how I can remove those feelings.

And to be honest with myself I can't. I have tried so many times. I changed my mind once, so I decided to come here to this island by myself. I never understood why I needed to come so far in an attempt to comprehend which words and feelings I couldn't possibly understand.

I'd missed many important moments of my life and moments with people around me; but I can't say that they were all crucial moments. I came to this Island to remember that day when I was inside a dark civilization. I remember these voices around me, someone held my hand in this bright room.

Everyone talked softly and sometimes flashy and a little off-balance. I was so young I didn't know exactly what happened in the room. I felt this was definitely not a good thing but I hesitated to ask many questions. Also, I was thinking that I could choose my own assessment later. However, I was hidden in the basement.

I felt like a piece of dust that the system (people) used many times day by day; and after you were thoroughly exhausted they promptly trashed you.

I have enjoyed many good times in life, where I felt important like I could reach people's minds and understand their feelings in many different situations and places. Everyone was setting off for special and new duties, always with a new evaluation and full of big and sometimes frightening vocations. Every day life outside treated us with no emotion, no feeling. As time passed, we as a group felt disconnected. The night after you fell into a very troubled sleep it offered a few hours of , momentary comfort until the next day, but every day we had to follow with dread.

Being here I have never felt loneliness so close to me. But I started to feel as a human being miserably responsible to become my own closest friend and my own support, and understand my vision and my capacity.

And then was GOD with me, with my heart broken, my time running low, my feelings to share with God. He was there and he is still around me all the time. Sometimes I felt as if my nerves were electrified, but I still knew God was with me. There were moments at the Island that I couldn't understand me and sometimes things inside me, and I've been known to wonder who would come inside my life and try to live my life—who would do that? I gave it a chance for all this to happen or offer an opportunity to change attitudes and take actions ... I changed my life; that was simple. I remember many happy moments when I was changing so much, but I'm here and I know what changes I made to myself to get past the craziness.

My mind is clearer, no weakening thoughts. No judgment, and my mind wasn't blanking out as often as before. I thought maybe I was all ready to return. Or maybe I could stay longer so I can understand why I'm here on this island alive. Wait one moment; I didn't know how exactly I'd arrived here – It had been four weeks by myself; at this point I should know how I've changed and how I get out of here? I looked around the tiny house, it seemed that I had been sleeping for many years. I opened the door, went outside, and gazed at everything around my little house. It was all real. I smiled and looked for some faces, looking to hear some voices, and I thought something was not right... I was experiencing a slight discomfort. And then I realized that I was by myself , no sign of any fingerprints around, no sign of human beings around my small house. But as I kept walking, I heard voices and I knew that there were creatures around.

Walking slowly and confidently, I saw someone, and I felt hands on my shoulders.

I started crying and panicked with weird thoughts and worries. I couldn't tell anyone. I begged myself, "Please, I don't want to think anymore about this thing. I couldn't allow those thoughts to cause fear in my life and let this all become a disappointment. It's the worst thing to feel unworthy in the eyes of God, your friends, your family.

As I've said before, it wasn't the first time that I felt like that. When I was little, I remember having doll that was my friend and could also be my mother. The communication was not real and did not form a safe environment between us. My mother told me at the time that Marcia was a real person and my doll was just a toy. And she apologized always at the time because she didn't want me to feel more sadness. I always corrected her saying, "She is not a doll; she is Marcia, my little friend."

I still had brief moments in which I recalled that my mother checked me all the time to make sure that I was fine. She always said, "I love you and you'll be fine; Marcia is fine and you should be fine and be happy with other friends."

I said, "Mother, do you think Marcia has many friends?"

"Yes," she said, "and you should have many friends too."

Sometimes I felt very upset about my past. I wondered whether anyone else felt the same. I was very upset with words that didn't come out with my clear intent. I immediately brought the questions to the whole family from the moment I knew they would talk about it.

People are good, but some people can be very bad, my father said. "If you have a real and good friend, you do not need money. Have money and don't have a friend, your personality will be so mixed and troubled. Stop in your tracks as soon you realize that your 'best friend' treats you as spoiled purple cheese with a limburger odor. Break off the friendship before you realize that you've lost control.

I knew my father didn't have much money but he had a lot of good friends. In the middle of the conversation, I had a momentary reminder of my guilt. I promised myself I'd never put myself in anymore dangerous situations. And now I had many moments that urged me to say sorry to my family. It was very hard to let it go and admit, "Sorry, it was my fault."

My father, sisters and brothers said nothing, which made me feel they really loved me. At the moment with this feeling, I felt a warm hug from each one, which did seem real, but they didn't speak.

I felt strange, but I was also relieved it was over. Since that day I never talked about my cousin. Not a single word, nor about my father's family.

My life after that seemed to be missing something ... I could see in my eyes that I had failed a bit. I wanted to forget and to be proud of myself again. My family always brings some kind of comfort to me by telling me something was not my fault and the mistakes made were not even to be acknowledged. Remember, bad people make mistakes and always seem to try blame someone closer and preferably inaudible.

IDENTIFICATION SEARCH

23

It happened with the sun penetrating my complexion as if it were a focus of light so strong that I could not resist. I told Mariana that the day would contain news. She, without understanding anything, told me that she hoped it would be a good fall. Mariana as we knew her was the crazy type, liked to live more freely with many adventures and without anyone to deal with as she lived She stated, "I do not like to be suffocated, not even when I'm in love. I like to dream alone."

But it was the middle of May, that I really came to believe Mariana's feelings. She surprised me the moment she told me that what hurt her the most was liking pain too much."

I didn't know what to say, but I didn't believe it. Mariana was always present and cool, even if others didn't know her personally.

Now and then, someone in the group made a new friend, and introduced her to us. These girls, named Amarin and Darlin, were super social Japanese. They lived their lives very straight even if they may have wanted to say how much they'd like to be different. I told Darlin that she should be more relaxed, but she didn't care about that life.

I said, "Really?"

They just wanted to buy clothes and more clothes. Darlin was very friendly, yet at times there were occasional hours of sadness. But, when we got involved at the bar and dancing she became very excited. She never went out by herself, but I understood that it's too boring to be at the bar by yourself. To tell the truth, it wasn't until my late 20's that I found that though most of my friends were sincere, they were almost all troubled also. It's hard to live with people who don't care about the feelings of human beings; not necessarily that they're distant from each other. Whatever their attitude, sometimes they were simply scared.

As my father used to say about friends, "You don't buy each other, conquer each other, or deceive one another. That's when you realize that you can really help some." Anyone with a functioning mind must try to help their friends think clearly and righteously.

After many years I gave space to meet a young man with whom I could feel comfortable and I could trust again, Francisco. Today we are a little distant but still feeling a special affection for each other. Meeting people is my high-quality attitude. I remembered Paulo, a guy that I met at college, who suddenly disappeared for a week. He was seen as the tourist of the class. On Mondays, Paulo was moodily reviewing lowdown things that happened during the weekend. I introduced him to Mariana. What a crazy couple. He was delighted with the beauty and sympathy of Mariana. Soon I found that Paulo is the youngest of the family, farmer father, everything in hand. Paulo was Francisco's cousin and often he seemed in another world.

24

When Francisco disappeared, I discovered later the true reasons involved, including the search for his twin sister, but also for drugs. Francisco was not the type of needy person who demonstrated his feelings on his shirt sleeves. The family of Paulo and Francisco are Protestant and Mariana, Catholic. But growing up Catholic and going to church every Sunday, I didn't see any problem in Francisco embracing a different religion. It felt fine to me. Summer was turning into another fall when I met him. I shivered and felt as if there was a pact between us that had been fashioned specifically for us.

I felt that Francisco was like a little brother or son. I know that seems weird. But at the same time I felt a great passion but without explanation. I had never cared so much about someone. I felt worried about everything that was happening. I felt that it was transforming me, and I got sick when I disconnected from the moment. That is very crazy in itself. And sometimes I get help from a professional who can help me understand what's going on in and around me.

Things were changing around Francisco and me. When we took a break, I decided to separate. I was back to my hometown, the place I'd thought that I would not come back to anymore.

Francisco also returned to Curitiba and Paulo, to Fortaleza. After they finish classes, everyone separated. Mariana went back to Minas Gerais. Later Mariana accepted and understood that she no longer should feel guilt about her grandmother's accident.

With each day, I grew wiser and older, and not quite sure what my confusing feelings for Francisco were. Everything every day was a disciplined challenge to enjoy the moment.

Francisco and I were only about three miles away from each other. When the month of tests came, a few days before I traveled to Campinas, I met Paulo and asked about Mariana. They fought a lot, then broke up but returned—always returned.

I was waiting for Francisco. He was very ill and could not talk, though I really wanted to see him. I had been calling at his house but his mother or someone in the house always said that he was not home. Very strange and rude.

The next day, I waiting for Francisco at the bus station. He was supposed to pick me up.

Wow! What a drag! I couldn't wait any longer!

The city was packed, full of students from all over Brazil, the hotels, pension houses--everything was crowded. The Campinas courses were the best at the time. It was quite likely that we could find a place to stay. I was feeling stranded, but suddenly Francisco arrived at the bus station. I was waiting for him and he arrived at 7:00 am, a little bit late. From there we went to the pension' He stopped me on the road and said, "Lara, I need to talk to you urgently." Francisco was very dramatic when he wanted to talk.

I didn't believe it was so serious, anyway ... Why?" I asked.

Francisco asked, "Would you consider meeting my family?"

I didn't believe it. "I don't know, Francisco, I will think about it. He said, why do you look so uncertain? You don't want to go?"

"Yes," I said, "I want to go but I don't want to bother anyone.

He said, "You won't be a bother; my family just wanted to know about you."

25

This was on a Saturday, and I became restless, feeling strange sensations. When the night arrived, I called Mariana. We talked only a bit because she was already leaving for Campinas on a flight at 5:00 am. On Sunday, we went to lunch at the restaurant to eat Lebanese food; we love the taste of it.

It became very popular in Brazil "Habib's" which is currently the biggest Arabic fast-food franchise in the world and the third biggest fast-food company in Brazil. We asked for fried kibbeh. But we were tense due to the next day's tests that would start at 8:00 am. Everything went well until the next day. Mariana, as she already knew the city, took us to the college court and explained to me where the rest were supposed to be and in which block and room.

She would be at the high school building around the next corner. I said, "Good luck" to her and we moved on to our block. I finished the exams much later; the group was already waiting for me. They were staying in a hotel, because where Mariana and I were, there were far too many students. They preferred to stay at the hotel.

I followed on foot since the boarding house was near. When I arrived guess what I found? Francisco, I didn't believe it!

I said, "How did you find Paulo's place?"

"Sit down and I'll tell you how I got here. It was as if everything was planned. I walked into my classroom, finished the exams and went out to the college to pick you up, but to my surprise, I found Mariana on the wall feeling sick and tired. However it was a fitting encounter.

I asked, "Mariana, have you seen Paulo? Did you find him here? In what block?"

She said, "Number 8, room 19."

I didn't believe it. "I'm in block eight at room twenty."

She said, "Next to mine?"

I confirmed.

I said, "I want a big hug, because you can't even imagine how much I was looking forward to seeing you."

"I'm in love with you, Lara," Francisco said.

Francisco's father was Spanish and his mother

was French. Francisco traveled a lot to Portugal and made a declaration of love to me in both Spanish and French. It was not what I expected.

From that moment Francisco and I met every day. I felt something very special for him.

Not being with him for a while, I thought he had another girlfriend. We were together and at the time he had an affair with Lucia. I caught them having sex at Amarin's house. It was a big dilemma between the families. Francisco said he didn't like her; it happened because he wanted to, but he didn't love her and she knew it."

In fact, Francisco was afraid to love. Loving had put several things aside, such as his gang of hype and drugs and his incessant travel. But he was failing to let go. There was something about him. I also stated with bright and tearful eyes at the time of the entrance exam that Francisco was not in good health and neither was I. I cared so much for Francisco, but I had to travel to São Paulo after this and the test I would meet Francisco.

Francisco needed to undergo further tests, since by the turn of the year, he abused drugs and did not stop smoking. He finished his tests on Thursday. I left the same day at sunset, because I needed to spend several days at Rio de Janeiro to visit amiga. Francisco, Paulo and Mariana would stay to celebrate the birthday of their friend, Marta. Marta was one of the girls who lived in the pension. Francisco could only go on Saturday. He would be waiting for the result of the entrance exam and would take the opportunity to play guitar for the staff. He played super well and sang too.

That night was a great one. The next day, Francisco went away sad feeling great pain. In fact no one passed the test. Oops, I lied, Amarin had passed. The results came out on Monday morning, shaking everyone's confidence.

It took days and days for us to forget about the test failing. It was a deep sadness and it took a while to recover. Francisco and I continued to communicate daily. I started to understand his behavior and the relationship between Francisco and me was growing strong. There was something between the two, we communicated even at a distance; spiritism influenced both of . We felt a strong impact even far away.

26

I could feel the sensation that Francisco transmitted to me once in the house when I went to spend a few days in Campinas. It was unbelievable, and it was the same feeling that Francisco felt as well.

That next fall Francisco and I did an interview and were accepted at the company. We got into a good trust company with training in the business area. I was in line with the choice to work for the Software sector with a highly respected engineer. Francisco went to the area of finance and got work in the national bank. His main focus was the financial market infrastructure companies that were growing in Brazil, and it was also in the ranking for highly associated challenging work, a high level of responsibility, and an excellent reference for a future career that Francisco's eye was on.

In September 2002, Francisco and I went to Fortaleza to visit Paulo who was sick. When I arrived there was an unexpected surprise from Mrs. Isabel Torrone, Francisco's mother. I didn't expect to see her visiting Paulo also. She greeted me quietly and delicately with sincere words coming from her mouth, saying that she had already met me elsewhere, but at the time did not want to insist on the memory because she knew it was not convenient.

But the day passed and finally I went to Francisco's house. The full moon appeared, seemingly as a flash in the sky, bringing them closer to the balcony as I enjoyed a long chat with Madam Isabel.

Later, Madan Isabel got up and went to the room I was in and covered me with the sheet. It was cold and the window was partly open, and I fell asleep quickly. Madam Isabel looked at me and thought:

"I don't believe it; it can't be true what I'm thinking."

At breakfast Madam Isabel made sure that Francisco and I had a cafe together, so she could better observe the two of us together. In each observation I felt something strange and with great certainty that I was the daughter she was told had died in childbirth and only survived Francisco. I was another baby, but the doctor gave us still another infant to bury. It was all happening so fast.

At that moment I was with my biological mother and my brother. My thoughts were back from my ancestry; no, it couldn't be.

It was the twin babies who were in front of Madam Isabel after almost thirty years.

Madam Isabel became "my mother." She felt that she would have twins, and when it came time for birth, two babies were born, a boy and a girl, only the female surviving.. Madam Isabel always said that the two would be alive and that when the girl appeared, there had been a mistake. Madam Isabel believed that she had finally found her daughter.

27

Madam Isabel was betrayed by the people, the family, but deep inside she found a way to believe very deeply and in every living atom of her body, a surety that she had found her daughter.

Francisco's mother needed to search for the truth about her biological daughter. She read in the news that thousands of children were taken from hospitals and sold to wealthy families. She believed that this was what happened to her daughter. Once Isabel had returned from the hospital, exhausted and very sad, her husband was careful. He neither wanted to talk nor to forget the twins. He had a vision that his daughter was alive somewhere, but he couldn't talk about these issues because Isabel was in a state of non-acceptance of the reality unwilling to accept any evidence but her own. Sr. John had the right to continue in silence. Isabel couldn't imagine that her husband had the same idea. I didn't assume anything; otherwise she would think he had to find their daughter.

During the months of total silence, Sr. John had hinted that their daughter had been sold. As mentioned, at the time many babies had been sold outside of Brazil. He remained mystified and very confused, and his thoughts grew more vague every day.

He hadn't different images and Madan Isabel was delivering the babies; he remembered a doctor giving him a cup as soon as the babies were born. But sometimes he thinks the cup of something was given to him before the babies were born. Three months passed and each month seemed longer because Isabel made the days comfortable for Francisco. He needed to be loved and nurtured as a child could be from his parents. With happiness, and with this tiny baby boy the pair started to focus on him. They organized his room—everything with lots of love. But the resistance between me and my daughter was strong and in spite of the life inside me, always there was a little hole of sadness. My daughter's room was made from rare wood with crafted etchings. The crib was beautiful and her clothes were so small and soft. All her things felt like silk satin. Isabel's mother made the crib cover by hand with a special design of intricate flowers and matching little bears.

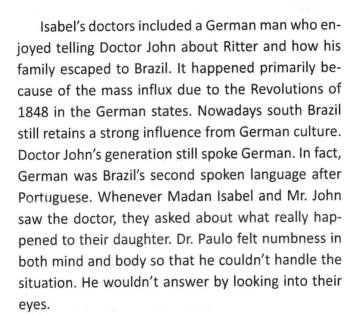

Isabel's doctors included a German man who enjoyed telling Doctor John about Ritter and how his family escaped to Brazil. It happened primarily because of the mass influx due to the Revolutions of 1848 in the German states. Nowadays south Brazil still retains a strong influence from German culture. Doctor John's generation still spoke German. In fact, German was Brazil's second spoken language after Portuguese. Whenever Madan Isabel and Mr. John saw the doctor, they asked about what really happened to their daughter. Dr. Paulo felt numbness in both mind and body so that he couldn't handle the situation. He wouldn't answer by looking into their eyes.

He changed the subject soon and began discussing a new medication innovations.

"I am not Madan Isabel's daughter, my legitimate parents are Nancy and Joao Alberene and I have six siblings."

After this visit to Francisco's parents, we did not see each other anymore for a while. I only spoke by phone with Francisco and his parents.

Paulo's illness continued, requiring several cardiac examinations that left Mariana very sad and worried. It was a week without news of him. I came to visit then on summer break. I went to Madam Isabel's house with Francisco and some friends who worked with him. Francisco's parents had a nice huge house and they didn't care that Francisco brought friends and threw a big party.

One late night after a party, they called me saying that Mariana had suffered a serious accident on the road. I went as fast as I could to the hospital. There was my friend, motionless, with braces, serums, and what-not. I was very nervous, I had to cry to be able to vent and I had only the strength to stand next to Mariana but the painful facts did not stop there. At the same moment, I called Paulo to warn him of the accident. He wasn't close by; he had just been removed to São Paulo, where he would be admitted to the Siri Lebanese hospital. I was desperate. I could not tell her about Paulo but I could tell Mariana about Paulo. I was waiting for the doctor's visit to give me information about Laura's clinical condition so I could tell Paulo exactly what happened.

It was not the best hospital and Laura would be removed to Curitiba, a clinic specializing in spinal treatment. The orthopedist explained that she would have to be paralyzed, because there was a deviation of the nerve of the medulla and it was necessary to do an urgent surgery, but what we didn't expect was her state of unconsciousness to worsen.

She fell into a coma and was taken to intensive care because she needed a blood transfusion.

While my friend, Paulo, was having heart surgery in São Paulo, I was concerned about his recovery. I wanted at that moment to be at two residences simultaneously. It was not easy, I felt as if the sun was going to burn out, the moon seemed to dim forever and the stars would no longer shine. I thought that of all this that I once had, I was going to lose both, and I went into a state of such despair. It had been at least a week since the two of them were in intensive care.

Mariana left the Intensive Care unit headed toward the apartment, already in a less critical condition. Paulo was recovering even faster than Mariana. He already was in the room, and began to ask for her without knowing what exactly was occurring at the time, and Mariana began to ask for Paulo constantly.

Day by day they were both recovering very well. Paulo went to visit Mariana and they shared a long, passionate kiss in a tight and very affectionate embrace. There began the true romance that soon marked the date of the wedding.

They chose the date and place for the wedding;

it was beautiful and full of joy. Francisco was the groom's best man and I was the bride's maid of honor.

Getting prepared for Mariana and Paulo's wedding, we labored day and night. She picked the Church—a Hillsong and wanted to explain why she chose the Mount Healing in Sao Paulo. She said, "They basically helped me to get back to my education and didn't judge me." One of the members of the church said to me, "Here all people are well-accepted no matter their lifestyle, no judgment."

The Mount Healing Church was not too close to the reception, and some guests did rent a hotel room, and also cars for the ones who didn't live closer. Mariana's family stayed at the hotel for a week helping to prepare for the wedding. Her grandparents helped a lot with invitations, flowers, photographs in the church. Paulo took care of the reception cost and honey-moon. Everything was beautiful. Mariana's brother walked the bride down the aisle. She was so pretty. All the bridesmaids were dressed in sky blue, the groomsmen's tuxedos were sky blue and the blazers were white.

I felt very happy because of moments of pure joy for Mariana. After the ceremony, I finally was able to be with Francisco, and I heard him say softly, "I was thinking that the next wedding, you will be the one walking down the aisle and I will be there waiting for you."

I didn't even respond correctly; I was tired after helping Mariana for a few days with the wedding. My level of energy was a little bit down at the moment.

"Did you hear me?" Francisco said.

I said, "Yes," And I hugged him and I said, "I've really been missing you too."

I wanted to be honest and say, "I love you and I want to spend all my time with you," but I was quiet. I didn't want to seem premature.

We all drove to the reception that was very close to the hotel. I was able to stop and grab some things that I took with me and I made sure all my belongings were out there. So, it was Mariana's room and all the bridesmaids were together in one big suite. The special suite room would be replaced for Mariana and Paulo.

Francisco said, "The hotel manager already replaced all the girls' luggage."

"The room is ready for the bride and the groom, Mr. and Mrs. Oliveira. I'll bet that everything looks very romantic,"

I said to Francisco. "I just want to see how it looks, but I don't have the key anymore."

Francisco held my hand, and we went to his room and found my luggage was there. Anyway I knew because the managers already knew where to put each specific piece of luggage and with whom.

Mariana asked, "Where have you guys been?"

I said, "I had to stop by at the hotel; it was quick."

And she said, "Let's dance and drink." I was relaxing a lot and Francisco and I danced the whole night, and of course we got a little drunk.

Well, I told Francisco, we just mixed some drinks and we know that will be a big problem tomorrow. He said, "I am not worried about tomorrow," and then kissed me." I was not expecting the kiss. But I responded very well.

The party was over at 3:00 am. Carlos, Lucia, Roberto, Ricardo, Carla, Ana, Francisco and I were almost the last ones to leave the big saloon. I noticed a group by the bar, and guessed they were Paulo's family and the friend that came from Portugal to cheer them on.

It took a long time to realize that I really loved Francisco and I did not want to lose him again. I really needed to be strong and not let Franscisco's mother be in control any more.

My romance with Francisco became more clear and real. I was more relaxed and flexible about the possibilities of the marriage with Francisco and having a family.

Francisco and I finally had a sense of not running again from each other. Neither found excuses or threw out problems that we could not solve , and also we were not giving anyone the right to ruin the future of our marriage. But anyway I wanted to do one more thing before I moved and settled in with Francisco, and I was all ready to tell him the full truth about my cousin and Mariana and everything.

I already confronted Mariana, and she said, "I will prepare myself with the help of therapeutics. I need to express my hurt feelings for many years against Alfonso, and I deserve to be out of this desert of dry feelings, that do not go away. I deserved a better quality of life; Mariana felt that she was out of control in her life and she already wanted to look for help."

Mariana quickly retained a lawyer, very well known. It was a woman, Mrs. Cote. She had been a lawyer for about twenty-five years and had much experience regarding Mariana's cause and mine too.

Mariana called me and gave me the news about her decision,

"Well done, I'm all ready also" I said to her on

the phone. "I've been waiting for this moment for a very long time."

"Me too, it will make me free. How about you?" she asked.

"Yes, and I hope we'll be fine! "I said.

"Don't worry."

"Well, should I get a lawyer too?"

Mariana said, "You don't need to have a lawyer."

My words all tumbled out at once, "It was me with my order to throw all the beach rocks along the cliff's shoreline, because I knew Alfonso always jumped at the same spot." I wanted him to get hurt too. He didn't die from the fall, but got hurt pretty bad, and his injuries contributed to his death later,"

Yes," I said, "he officially died from cancer!"

And she said, "All these things make me very concerned."

"If you can be there at the court it would help," she said. "Can you?"

I responded, "Yes, of course!"

"I want to be all ready to confirm everything about what he did to " us."

Mariana was very anxious, and she didn't want to get there too early. I arrived a half hour before her. Francisco and Paulo were there with us. They gave all the support they could. We and also our family were there for us. I saw my parents and Mariana's brother also present. I can't even describe my feel-ings, which had been filled with hurt for many years and Mariana faced the same. Sometimes, both of us wanted to be free and without holding a responsibil-ity that was not our fault. We wanted to get all the beautiful feelings back.

After a few days in trial court, with fearful mo-ments and high anxiety, I couldn't quite stop the trembling.

"It was a mistake to be here," I said to Francisco.

He said, "No! You think it is a mistake to be here. No, it's about you; you deserve to be free and they deserve the truth."

"I hated him," I said.

Finally, the trial was over and Mariana was judged not guilty, and everyone should have un-derstood that Mariana had a reasonable excuse for hurting Alfonso.

But w you did things that put him in a wheelchair. That's not what some people at the time thought was the correct way to bring retribution. And my aunt said, "Alfonso is not here to defend himself." She added, "You're here, walking and alive."

Mariana and I could not respond to my aunt because our thoughts clashed with hers. "We both know that her son was a monster and didn't de-serve our forgiveness," I added, "I hope that my aunt prayed for her son to be in a good place, even though he did not deserve it."

At the trial, Mariana's therapist and her lawyer came to testify and the big surprise was that Mariana did not commit any crime.

"They were telling me in court that Mariana asked for the guys to do the job. However, the services were not done because those guys were caught before, serving at the bar where they fought. Then they'd stay the whole night in jail. So, no rocks were put on this specific spot where Alfonso always jumped. Mariana Albergo was not guilty, as no law enforcement file showed extra rocks were added at the edge of the cliff where Alfonso usually jumped. Unfortunately, what happened with Alfonso was purely an accident.

Mariana said to me, "That's not true."

I said, "What?"

"I paid the two guys later; they said they did the services. "So who was right or who was wrong in this court?"

I said to Francisco, "That's good, at least Mariana didn't feel so miserable thinking that she did a horrible thing."

And Francisco said, "Alfonso got what he deserved for being a cruel rapist."

I like the way he responded.

And I added," People think that they can do what they want and there should be no consequences, and many wrong things fade in the pale. They pretend that guilt vanishes like wind, but the hurricane will turn around and catch them on the day they least expect the worst to happen.   I tend to think what my parents would say, "Things happen the way they're supposed to."

I felt very disconnected with their point of view, and I didn't support their thoughts about it.

My mom said, "Your opinion is always basic on information regarding your heritage and you say that it will always support your final decision."

I replied, "There's always a little debate on various matters, and I hope I can change my mind at some point."

Francisco's mother finally accepted me after Francisco asked me to marry him. But, before, she did everything possible to separate her son from me, I thought that she would never want to meet me. I had a change of mind one day and decided to be at the house for their anniversary. Francisco had asked me so many times to be there with them.

I said, "I knew that you would invite me to go,

but I know there is no reason for me to be there with your parents. I also know that your mother doesn't want me to be there.

"Maybe she thinks that I took her son from her."

Plus I looked so much like Francisco, sometimes people that didn't know we were together would ask if we were brother and sister. And then I'd have to explain things all over again." "One day I said, "We are twins." The word twins came out of my mouth very spontaneously.

Francisco looked at me and said, "Please never say that again."

Since that day I never have used the word twin to describe us. I should have been more careful, and of course at the time I didn't know the whole story about Francisco's baby sister. But I knew that he had a sister and the sister died a week later. That's what I thought before I met Francisco.

Francisco's mother still seemed hopelessly looking for her daughter, and one day somehow I must have given her the impression that I was her daughter. . Francisco traveled a lot, and moved from city to city for work, prepared to finish his training. So Francisco could make six to nine big trips in one year.

Of course, weeks dragged by without seeing him.

Thus, Francisco hadn't much time for his mother either. I asked Francisco about his mother, who'd been alone all this time, and he said she'd actually run away from reality. Then time passed so fast and she didn't seem to notice that you'd departed in a new direction and that at some point your father was running away too. I asked Francisco, "When your father stayed longer in Portugal, was he running away from the situation, because of your baby sister or because of your mother? Didn't your mother have a breakdown for a long time?"

Francisco said, "I believe that was true of both situations. Neither has my mother asked him how he felt overall about his daughter." Francisco added, "My father felt so guilty about it; he was devastated. He didn't even ask to see the tiny baby girl's body."

When he put himself together it was simply too late to bring back my twin baby sister. And I was there waiting to be nurtured and be loved by my parents. As for myself, Francisco told me that he was keeping his own problems to himself. I had a little problem trying to learn fast because I always pretended to be stronger so my parents needn't deal with me. My father was there for me occasionally; my mother, I can say yes, but only in the way she could deal with it. I had accepted the way everything was.

I said to Francisco, "I really don't understand why your mother needs to feel guilty. And didn't we take care of you better?"

I said, "No, I am sorry to say it like that," and I cried, then hugged Francisco. I continued, "What I want to say is, 'Your mother sees you there with everything around you: good food, nice house, money there to buy what you need, and then she thinks about your sister, what she is doing now, if she is fine or not.'

I stared out the window, "I believe that she couldn't handle all the stress, and seeing you there, of course, her feelings, thoughts, and her eyes yearned to one day see your sister, her baby daughter that she still believes could be alive...but where?"

Francisco said, "Yes, she felt all that."

———— ∞∞∞ ————

Francisco and I were walking one day and we passed across this big bridge that goes through to another side with a lot of construction materials. It seemed that someone would build this edifice or house. We were not sure exactly but the area was big. While we crossed the bridge, Francsico was telling me that when he was at a young age--around four, he started asking his parents, "Why does my cake have two names and colors? It was a big and beautiful cake—one side decorated with flowers, angels, and the other side decorated with a horse or birds. At the time, it was the two animals that I liked most on top of the cake. I always asked for a snake--that was the third animal in which I was very interested,

Francisco said to me. "My mother never wanted to decorate my cake with a snake."

I asked why, and he said, "She is very afraid. When she was age sixteen, a snake bit her very badly, but luckily the snake was not a poisonous one. In any case she got traumatized by any kind of snake." And the other side, I loved the idea of having a pet-friendly snake anyway. He said, "And always the cake was made--one part in pink named Fabiola and the other part in blue, Francisco.

"I couldn't understand why every year had to be the same. I asked my mother why? "I remember,", Francisco said, "I was four years old and she told me, 'we celebrate your twin sister who is not here now but she will be one day'."

And every birthday was the same, until I turned fourteen. I told my mother that I didn't want anymore celebrations of my birthday and I did not want cake or anything anymore." Francisco continued, "I felt I was not there. I understand my mother found it very hard to not let a child go whom we never saw and every day feeling that your child is alive. That feeling was between us for many years. At this point my mother has to be in peace, we did everything that was possible and even 'impossible' to find my little sister. I understand that it's very difficult, but we can try to become almost everything about my sister but it will never bring her back."

After a brief moment of silence my heavy breath broke the silence as we continued walking across the long bridge. We knew that the weather was supposed to change later and quickly the sky turned dark with storm clouds signaling an impending torrent. Since early that morning we had noticed the shower would come later according to the forecaster. So, I asked Francisco, "Do you want to walk back or continue in a cab."

He responded, "I do not mind continuing to walk but first shelter for a bit under the bridge, if you don't mind. Do you?"

I said, "Not at all, I love being on the railing."

And then he said, "Sometime when I was younger—about ten years, I usually stayed for hours under the bridge by my house, not exactly to close and I stayed there especially on the days of my birthday and Christmas, and mother's days, because it seemed that I could bring back so many memories of my parents, but I didn't think those memories were…happy moments."

I held Francisco's hand tied my knuckles went white and I stopped first by his side and very quickly

I moved in front of him and I hugged him very tight as he realized that was a lot of love there.

Marrying Isabel's son was the greatest challenge of my life, and my most taxing time for patience. And outside of my relationship with Francsico, I had my heart and broke down feelings because of my cousin Alfonso. I thought, Francisco's life would be better if he did have to carry his sister on his shoulder every moment that his mother lives. It was clear that Dona Isabel, every time, was gazing at Francisco growing and becoming a handsome young man. She stood beside him and said, "Your sister could be here side by side with you. And I knew Francisco did not like to hear this, and at one point, he told me "I can't handle my mother around me, because I believe that she is constantly seeing my sister and not me."

Now, I wonder, how could Fransisco have ever enjoyed his own life without being compared to his sister? I asked Franscisco one afternoon, "Do you feel you were abandoned or treated as simply 'moments of relief' for your parents, especially your mother?"

He said, "My mother's feelings toward me disallowed herself from valuing my love. I was there every second and every minute, but I believe she was thinking about my sister all the time, permitting no space to see me,"

After a short downpour, but enough to get both of us sopping wet, the only way was walking back but it didn't take long.

I remember walking with Francisco. He was holding my hand, and also supporting my decision to select the church, flowers, place for the reception, and where we should live after marriage.

I asked Francisco, "Do you not want to live around your parents, since you are the primary one from the family around?"

He said, "Don't worry, I believe the wisest plan is to move closer to my grandmother in Portugal. I am not sure," said Francisco again, then went silent.

Those days Francsico saw his mother as nearer to him. Less comparisons; she didn't mention a lot about his sister in a way that made him feel abandoned, at least not as much as she did before. She tried to look at him as her only child.

Francisco said another day, "She seems to be doing brilliantly,. She has cried all her tears away thinking about my sister. But I believe that she still cries and will never stop thinking about my twin sister. She has recognized after many years of therapy that she'd navigated for so long with her own boat and one day she thought she could not return. She realized that she needed Franscisco and she wanted to grab back all the time that she'd let slip away. She had missed so much her baby girls, at every moment of every day, there was little light and joy remaining to enjoy. Even though Francisco's father and Francisco were there with her all the time, too much of the time she was off walking aimlessly looking for a miracle.

The day of the wedding, the sky was clear–not too hot. We decided to not have a big party, not like Paulo and Mariana. But it was beautiful and astounding almost until the entire night turned to day. We celebrated the whole night. It was a big reception at the hotel, so no one had to drive far from the church because the church was so close. My sisters and my friends, and aunts, uncles, my mother, everyone walking, and while they were walking to the church they threw petals of flowers. So, my pathway was already made very beautiful with all different colors

The photographer did a good job taking thousands of photos. In front of me and my father was Mariana's daughter, Amanda, who was five, and she was carrying Francisco's wedding ring, and Francisco's cousin Dane, seven years of age, and he was carrying my wedding ring. Behind them I was walking with my dad. It was a nice conversation. He said, "Are you happy?"

And I said, "Yes, father," and he said, "I am very happy for you, very proud dad that now sees my daughter very smart and very free from the past. You grew up with many challenges, with the silence as your best friends, and with a heartbreak, but today you finally accepted your heart was fixed and it will be for forever."

And my father continued, "I am so sorry that I was not there at the time you needed me the most."

And I said to my father, "You should not be ashamed, neither should mum, because of people's sickness. And your sister, my aunt, I felt sorry for her for not understanding her son's behavior."

We didn't get longer into the conversation for the reason that I didn't want to completely unrobed these memories on my special day, and plus I'd already solved the problem. I should look more at how I would take good care of my future. I should get up every day happy with Francisco by my side, happy with acquaintances around me to do the same.

I left behind friends and family, then today I found my marriage with a tiny taste of my lore that I thought I left behind; Francisco now takes a different approach about my past and respects my decision, that on a certain day I have to experience and understand why it is so important to embrace your genetic traits.

I said to Francisco, "I thought you'd have the same feelings for not following in your father's footsteps?"

Francisco 'hated' that's not the exact word, but he had been working for his father and always complied almost like a ten-year-old. And he's never stopped working with his father. Then he said, "It is a good tradition that involves a lot of things. I see myself explaining things, almost exactly as my father did, and one day, my mother said, "You talk like your father."

"The coincidental behavior all will be there." I said to him, "You don't have to be a carbon copy of your father; if you wish create your own personality authentically."

Behind my limits and many changes, I remembered very well the last meeting I had with Mariana and Paulo. As soon as they married, they went on a trip. And I shared with them that I had been a twin baby were a baby boy and a baby girl.

I said to her, "Those babies are the most beautiful gift I would have in the world. Donna Isabel, the grandmother, could spend many hours with the twins; she never missed any birthday celebration, Christmas and she made everything perfect never missing any events related to the twins. Mariana asked me, "Is it true that "your mother in law always offer trips to you and Francisco, so she can spend long hours and days with the twins?" Mariana continued, "Do you think that your mother-in-law replaced the twins so she wouldn't miss her baby girl too much?"

"Yes," I said, "I believe her son's twins, covered a huge empty hole that had been in them almost forever, and the twins came to replace the gap of her twins and her grandchild in an effort to raise a completely happy family.

AT THE TIME OF FAREWELL

28

I don't remember very well the exact day of that party; I just remember it was in the month of October. It was a party that lasted an entire week, but in my recollection, lasted more than ten years. It's always very funny when I go back to this place. Not only me, but the whole class from high school. I determine myself to know more classmates. I was so busy with my small group that I did not have time or interest in seeing the whole class.

Lucia's was the daughter of the supervisor of the school. When I met them, I was embarrassed. Sometimes I was one of the last ones to leave from school. After the PE class practice, I liked to take a shower before going to my house. I once opened the door and stepped into the shower room. I saw Lucia's parents naked taking a shower. Oh my gosh, I was so embarrassed and confused and I left so fast that I believe they didn't see me. Luckless, Lucia was always by herself, had a crazy parent. I recall they loved to travel, and were always going on a long trip, sometimes it would take months because they even chose their itineraries by cruise ships steaming off to some European country.

When I was going to visit my father's sister who lived in Paraguay, I was sixteen years of age. My parents decided to visit one of his old friends at my house, and then they'd go shopping at the Paraguay shop, China Marketplace. Everything over there was cheaper, but I never was lucky with my shopping. A few days later the staff of a bough broke apart. My father always bought their tires, and my mother some food and perfumes, ice cream, and she always gave me a little money, so I could buy some stuff too. I remembered being so proud and very responsible to have my own wallet and money in my pocket. I liked the idea of walking around doing my own personal shopping; I could only buy what my money afforded. I was in love with this little music box. When I saw the price I was really happy because it was exactly the amount I had in my wallet.

So, I decided to buy it, then I went back to the other store where my parents were, and I asked my mother if it was okay to buy the music box. I had to ask because my parents just bought a big music box. So, maybe they'd complain about the noise. But I did end up with the music box; I just had to leave it in my room.

I said, "Of course, Mum." I remembered taking this music box everywhere. My brother's car didn't have a radio, so when I was in his car, I took my music box. It was fun.

After the shopping, it was about 3:00 pm, and we went to visit my parent's old friend. We passed the house twice; seems my father was lost. And he agreed, "Yep, I think we are lost!"

I didn't even listen much because I was trying to figure out how to use the music box. I finally opened it and notice that I needed batteries, so I would check. I forget, but usually no batteries were included. I was disappointed, and my mother said, "Those things never come complete, and she added, "I hope it works." Because we knew electronic things always had problems, the manufacturer is shoddy so damage in inevitable. I decided to put it back in the box; we were almost in front of my parents' friend's house.

I wanted to carry my music box inside the house.

My father said, "They have a daughter your age, when we arrived, which was more than thirty minutes, with no intention to be late. I looked at the girl, but I didn't know her name. Suddenly I realized I had heard her name before...Lucia. When I saw her mother, I recognized her from school. I had opened the shower and saw them taking a shower and I just knew that grin on their faces reflected their memory of my pie eyes when I saw them stark naked.

But I never put together the fact that Lucia was the daughter of the cantina people's owner. I let myself completely ignore that I knew them. I could have spoken to Lucia, but I didn't. I thought I would be so embarrassed, but Lucia, she might have a different perspective on me. I always liked to pray with Lucia at the school, but she was a little girl at the time.

We sat in the living room at Lucia's parent's house. They had a big home.

Lucia came to Paraguay because her parents needed to take care of the house while the grandparents visited; her grandparents pretended to move back to some country in Europe.

I was reminded when I saw her that we once talked about going to college one day together. After six months, Lucia's grandparents returned to Paraguay, and they sold the house and returned to France. So, they were back in Sao Paulo, and Yes, both became best friends. I do remember how she loved being in the group. On those days it was hard talking about Lucia; we missed her a lot.

It was a desperation when we heard the news of the tragedy; the class was having a good time but this experience was so discouraging that we even thought of separating. It was horrible, I still remember it like it was yesterday.

29

O nce in class, Lucia, said to me that Ricardo was from another world," I did not understand anything of that story, since in philosophy class everyone has a theory of life, and it was with these theories that we decided to make that party. The idea came from Carlos to go to that hut near the Morro do Apocalypse, a very Bantu place. Mariana at first did not agree with the idea, because she thought it too far from the city and we would not return on the same day. It seemed that she foresaw things; so much so that when he went to Venice, she knew that he had arrived in a safe manner.

That night, Charles alone came in a hurry with a raincoat covering his left shoulder, and with his face all bruised. It was past 11:00 pm and he was knocking on the door. I wondered how Charles departed that night, yes because the party had already ended two hours earlier. There was a minor argument between Ricardo and Carlos but nothing serious. From that moment I thought that there was something in the air, something mysterious about the party.

Charles had gone out with some colleagues we didn't know. He left without telling anyone and his absence was not noticed except by me, for he was the one I wanted in that moment of pain and loneliness. That gang Charles met made our party a farewell forever. He was someone who suddenly arrived with a bit of sadness and nostalgic despair. It seemed the storm entered with loud gales as if the home were to be torn to pieces. And there were voices whispering in our ears, making us think that the wind was whisking us to another place even farther away. We couldn't take it anymore and Charles could only tell us that it was time to get back as soon as possible. Lucia desperately said that we had to go back to prevent Charles from dying. However, Lucia did not realize that the return was no longer so easy, and that Richard had already tried, but without any success. The road had widened so that overtaking anyone was not possible.

Charles's condition worsened further and Mariana and I went out in search of medicine. What we found in the search was medicinal tea leaves that Mariana said were 'good.' Anyway, the tea that had been made for Charles was not enough for his healing, and what· I saw in every face was sadness and despair.

It had been two and a half days and nothing of that situation had been resolved. Paula began to make a scene of hysterics, and Fabio said that he would not stay even another minute in that place, stating that it was a flimsy shanty. Paulo begged us to return home, while Mariana asked for calm. Lucia mentioned that someone should go out for help and cross the Morro do Apocalypse. At the same moment she decided that she would go herself, with the help of Mariana, Fabio and Lucia.

30

I remembered the trip... "Here we are going to the Morro of the Apocalypse," I said, "I'm a little scared to be honest. I've heard a lot of comments about the place, and people always talking about ghosts. And I don't know if all those comments are products of the imagination. I asked, "Have you guys heard about this place before; it seems people get scared because of apparitions?"

Charles said, "Nope, it's all imagination; people isolate places because of myths."

And, then I said, "These myths surrounding us can and control our thoughts, that passed from are descent."

We'd barely arrived at the house, and I was frightened with the spooky style of the place. The first night, the TV made a weird noise and then it didn't work anymore. So, no TV. Carlos and Lucia complained because they love watching television. They'd find comedies and watch them over and over, laughing most of the time. I didn't think them so funny. At the same time, Mariana came down and said, "Guys, I just broke a dresser drawer," and everyone paused.

The silence was uncomfortable in the Frick house. So everyone grabbed a drink and went outside. Paulo and Mariana got drunk pretty fast. They liked to drink hard liquor. And, I told them, "We guys can become monsters when we're wasted; so I can't understand why you both mix drinks for hours." Many conversations made no sense. It seemed that everyone was in outer space. I couldn't understand their conversation. Every word was overlapping, and we talked loudly. I did drink a few beers, but I thought that was fine. Not really, though, because I felt sick the next day—better described as a hangover. Charles said, "Have a double cup of coffee."

I said, "Good idea."

And Paulo said, "Drink one more beer," and we couldn't stop laughing..

Seemed that everyone woke up tired, and we all stayed at the place for the day. The morning passed quickly. We went to the beach, and in late afternoon

Paulo, Carlos and Francisco , wanted to go fishing. Carlos knew the best places to fish, so they decided that if they found any fishing gear they'd go to the north shore. So they went to looking in the basement. There they found: fishing rods and reels, fish hooks, and a package of fishing weights, plus some basic clothes, like some footwear, gloves, wader boots, and more stuff. Around 5:00 pm, they went fishing, and returned around 10:00 pm with three nice cod. And Mariana said, "Only three?"

Paulo nodded. "Not many fishes at the Coastline at this time of the year."

That evening Carlos cleaned the fish and did BBQ--very delicious and well-seasoned. The day passed calmly, and everyone enjoyed the place even though the small city was a little bit far.

That night I was tired and decided to go to bed earlier. I fell asleep quickly and alongside me was Francisco . But before long he went to check the door or something. I remembered, as soon as he left the room, something fell from the roof almost striking my face, but I felt it on my body. I saw the animal running quickly. It looked like a big rat or a small cat, or maybe a vampire bat.

When I saw the animal, whatever it was… my God, I screamed so loud, and everyone ran to see what happened. We couldn't fall back to sleep for a while.

Finally I went downstairs with Francisco and we slept on the sofas. But I stared at the roof and stairs almost the whole night. It was not warm and cozy.

Then I was thinking about the Blue, and how I could dig into my thoughts without thinking about falsehood stories.

I probably got more scared because I'd heard stories to the effect that many people died in this place. Charles looked at me and he said, "I never heard anything about that, but he began to describe that his ankle one day was bleeding, and his clothing was torn apart at this creep house. Everyone got so scared. Then I asked, "What happened? Was it a wolf or a creepy person?

Charles laughed, and he said, "No, he was with that lady who was married, and then her husband discovered that she'd been cheating with someone, and he followed her. When he found my uncle, he beat him so bad the guy almost died."

And I said, "I hope cheaters learned a lesson."

Mario said, "Doesn't anyone believe in a caring God. We are not going to die, we're here at this place to have fun."

And then Fabio said, "It's not the moment to talk about that."

Finally, we arrived at the place, "I was wondering about this place that Carlos found and was surprised it was not closer to the city."

There was a convenience store about fifty miles away.

Everyone was tired and soon fell asleep, knowing some would wake early. And Carlos was the one who knew the place. He had been here before, so he was the leader until we got to the Hill of the Apocalypse.

Mario tried to explain how things in the house work and near the house was a beautiful lake surrounded by high mountains–very pretty.

Everyone helped put things inside the old house, and shortly after we decided to walk a little bit just to check around.

They were going to cross the Hill in the morning, about 5:00 am, and even though they were worried about Carlos' state, they tried to make a go of it. The attempt to cross the Hill was only made due to Charle's weird state. We were very concerned about his reactions that night, and the conflicts between us were growing, because we could not find a way to learn how Carlos left that night and returned in that sorry state, saying that he had met some colleagues.

But in fact there was no one around that hill, and not even miles away. I don't really know how Mario discovered this place that was so mysterious. The hours were tense and the days were frightening. It was not easy to spend those days in frenzy at the Morro of the Apocalypse. Even those parts that were so beautiful seemed to become very sad and mysterious from that morning still we came across him looking for help.

Fabio slipped and tumbled down the hill, got all bruised, and as a result we had to carry him back to the hut. The despair in our family continued. Fabio didn't even move and the class was now hating every minute of it. Lucia complained so much that it was necessary to yell at her, and to shout so loudly that the world would hear, and also the people who might be looking for us would have heard. With that came several arguments as to where each one would like to be at that moment, and suddenly the tears on some faces made others feel a sense of despair.

It was exactly midnight, and the third day next to that Hill was approaching. Irene fell asleep, surprisingly in love. Ana too, then finally the whole class fell asleep in fitful dreams. The third day, by the way, was the worst of all—the day we decided to leave that place and go to the other side of the Hill. Maybe there we would find something to cheer us up, since we all wanted to get out anyway.

The situation was getting more and more serious and painful. We realized that Mariana no longer cheered us up and Irene was losing her balance and no longer had the patience to speak softly. Mario was embarrassed and very confused by all this, while Lucia and Ana Carla did not say anything. In this particular situation, Fabio wanted to walk in search of something, but could not walk. Poor Carlos was the one who was least able to help himself. His fever was so high that in his delusions he said he wanted forever to eat only his mother's cooking. We were going through difficult times, witnessing the foul conditions in which Carlos found himself.

"Three days of fever was a lot," Anne said, and she added that Charles was pretending in order to avoid work. He no longer seemed to want to fight for us to come back as quickly as possible. It also indicated that he didn't want to leave, that he was the mystery of the class so he couldn't explain what had happened that night: -

Despair gripped Hannah in a very brusque and determined manner. Was she going to find out what really happened that night? Why would Mario have taken us to such a mysterious place?

Lucia said, "There is someone out of the ordinary in that place. Someone wanting to play a game, or else a ghost that appeared only to Mario." Lucia began to talk about the fiesta. He asked Ricardo what had happened that night. Who was so furious as to quarrel with crazy Charles for going out alone when there was no one around?

31

No one noticed his absence, then suddenly we realized that Charles was not present. When Carlos came knocking on the door, the pressure began for Ricardo's side who were very scared and unresponsive, but the class wanted to know everything regarding Lucia, because they disagreed with the charges, and especially those against Ricardo.

A headache struck some so forcefully that we screamed in pain. Our heads seemed to be spinning out of place and no longer reacting in the same way. Suddenly everything was going dark, everything more confusing than before. We no longer realized what was weaving around us; it was all so misty that we could see nothing else, not even the true friendships we considered strong and loyal.

That place seemed to count on someone who wanted our unhappiness or even our death.

Everyone wondered why all that mystery for a simple farewell, and they told each other that this was the most unfortunate outing they had ever had.

Irene always said when the class was gathered, that the greatest misery of a human being was to destroy the fantasy of a dream. Richard was curious at Irene's utterance and asked her why such a sudden argument with that air of certainty. It made Ricardo think all day.

Thus, another night arrived full of mystery. Lucia fell asleep saying that all which was left was a real ghost, and one of them jokingly said, "So what are we waiting for?" For the first time in days everyone found it funny.

The sun began to shine through the cracks in the hut and among the vague outline of leaves the sun was seen penetrating the Moro of the Apocalypse. This day seemed to be better than the previous ones, as Fabio began to react, his legs growing stronger and firmer, his arm already healed. We were very happy, because Carlos was also showing signs of improvement. The sun really was great and made our heads think of something positive, and enabled us to see that the fights wouldn't get us anywhere.

32

remembered Ricardo saying no one was to blame for the situation, and everyone agreed. This made the class excited to leave that place. Ricardo said he would cross the Moro, whatever the cost, so we packed the backpacks in order to leave before dark, even though Carlos was not yet fully healed. At this point I began to think that Charles might have some very serious illness, but I had no idea what it might be. Mario knew a lot about Carlos' life and could possibly say something about his friend's state.

He was very sad when Charles's fever increased, but he did not mourn. I tried to get into it and he tried to avoid me, but it was clear on Mario's face that there really was something very serious about Charles' health. However, I realized that they had made a pact and that the truth could not be told under any circumstances. The only thing I could get out of Mario was that Charles was not a normal person and he didn't want to prolong the conversation afraid that I would guess or force him to tell the truth. The class was again in anguish.

The sunny day was starting to get dark again and the idea of leaving that place came to nothing but we sluggishly prepared once more. I felt Carlos' farewell at that moment but I could do nothing. Irene felt that the situation was not normal and said that Carlos could not continue traveling, so they decided that someone would stay with him, because it would not be easy to climb the Hill with Carlos in that state and the class made the right decision. Lucia said that we could not leave the three of them alone, but Ricardo tried to explain to Lucia that if we took Carlos in that situation, we would not have the slightest chance of going up the Hill and asking for help.

They were going to leave without our company, so I began to think I could talk to Mario about Charles; I was just waiting for their departure to get into it.

Ricardo and the gang would discover another walkway, since they no longer remembered the path found earlier. Another day passed and the longing grew more and more. The sun began to fade, giving way to the stars and a serene dusk.

In the morning they were going to leave and yes it happened. Carlos hugged the gang that was going to leave. Mariana and Lucia began to cry, feeling that Charles was not far from death. To avoid this, we would have to bring a mobile medical unit to take him to a hospital to be properly medicated. It was difficult to say goodbye, because everyone was feeling that Charles would want very much to live. At about 11:30 a.m., Charles died in front of Mario who went out of control and screamed: "The world is very unfair, everything is wrong; what I will say to everyone?"

33

Unfortunately, Charles had left us forever in front of the Morro do Apocalypse. At dusk the class returned and I saw in their eyes that something good had been done. Indeed, Richard had found a way that would lead us to the nearest town. They were happy to know that we would leave that place. Ricardo and Ana said: "Now yes, we can save our friend. He will stay in a great hospital and his family will take very good care of him. "That's right," Fabio and Lucia agreed. Irene decided to wake him up and tell him the news.

I pulled her by the arm and felt the tears falling down my face, and with that the class soon realized everything.

Terrified, they asked Mario what had actually caused the death, but he couldn't say anything. So, Irene approached the body of Charles and said weeping: "He is dead."

And what we were left with was longing, sadness and many tears at the Hill of the Apocalypse.

The mystery continued, and so did the dreams that are part of life. In every brain the retreat of the Apocalypse works. Charles' death was on the rise, but he had stage one AIDS. How did we survive? Most of us had gotten so close to Charles.

We wanted to know exactly what happened at the cabin. And of course, the police investigation and interrogations continued for a week or more. Mario, it seems knew what would happen at the morro but all those years he didn't say anything. The police didn't find anything that showed any kind of violence between us. The only things were moments of heavy sadness and worry as we returned to the city. During the investigation the police found Mario most quiet of all prisoners and wanted all the time to be alone. At this time the ambulance and more police were at the Morro unable to find anywhere on the Apocalypse Hill. After five hours of investigation that had been also outside the cabin they could not see any sign of anyone or anything unusual around the morro.

Nothing could be investigated completely because Charles couldn't cooperate with the police. But Carlos' baby needed to rest and be at peace there with us. The enforcement and prayers were that all the rest would leave alive from the Hill before this sad accident happened. The situation had taken us through so many tears and discomfort and forever an empty and broken heart.

An old friend had always said, "Some people are here just for a visit and had the time to place themselves into a perfect moment, and this moment is the only present form to show before they die and the point is that some of those people who die early have already finished what needed to be done with and sometimes they had been sitting and waiting to chill."

And that was a weird thought, but it was also true that Charles had fulfilled his life goal early, though it was very sad. We all had to sign a document the police gave to us— including information about each one of us and the file of each one and a date and time to show at the police station in the city, which I already didn't like. I had stopped at the police station before because of my cousin's false accusations a few years ago. Before that, my life was so fine and I had been sitting by him and going to the beach on the day my heart was pumping.

34

"It's possible that the police will ask again about my case," said Mariana who knew what happened because she was there. She looked then said "Don't worry, you didn't do nothing; unfortunately, you have been so close to both and at the wrong time," Thus I knew what the police would ask me all over again.

"I feel strange," Laura said, "the police are looking more toward Ricardo and Charle's arms that seem wounded from a fight last night. I said, "Really, that doesn't make sense and it does not prove anything.

She simply d, "I don't know. Maybe they know something that we don't." She looked into my eyes and said, "Maybe one day Mariana saw something strange in Ricard's eye that day which sounded an alarm."

I intentionally made myself talk to Ricardo. I said, "Hey, Ricard."

For a minute he didn't respond.

I again, said, "Are you hearing me?" and we exchanged a look.

I could feel his pain.

He said, "I'm lost and very mad for not caring better for my friend."

I tried to say something. He raised a trembling hand. "I don't know what I could have done."

I was with him in the room and he seemed fine."

"There is something that I need to tell you" and of course the silence settled in a place inside of me. I had held my breath listening to Ricard, and he tried to move clumsily around me to check with someone moving closer to us.

I suddenly understood the seriousness of the conversation. "How did you know that and how did you hear?"

Ricard spoke slowly, "I heard someone talk to Carlos about his disease."

"And Carlos was in silence? You didn't hear any reply from Carlos?" I asked.

"No," Ricard said … "He hadn't even said a word. I don't think he wanted us to know."

"Do you think that Carlos too died because of this illness?"

"No, please, I don't know, and never tell anyone I told you this."

"I said, "Don't worry, but we need to know and to test all of us, don't you think?"

"Yes... Yes. Let the police and the hospital confirm the truth to everyone."

At that moment, I started to think about the AIDs and we were all together, I mean in the same house and taking care of him. Without precautions..." I was starting to panic.

As the words left Ricardo's mouth, I started feeling quite sick. I know the psychologist spoke in my head and my heart began again to beat faster, my hands cold. Ricardo said, "Relax, no one had contact with Carlos in a way which would cause any danger regarding the disease. Let's stay calm."

"What if he transmitted to someone from here? You didn't know? Maybe he did not either for sure? I was so desperate. I would explain to myself my worries and I didn't care if I needed to tell the nurses to do the right examination. I knew that I didn't need to wait for the final result from the doctors. "He," they said, "he died from something else." I wanted to know the truth and I was going to take the test, and I did, and so did everyone else.

I became worried about everyone, and I started doing my research about AIDS and the differences of

HIV. I wanted to be educated about this. It seemed that everyone knew about AIDS, and of course everyone knew that it's a danger and a very serious disease, and according to the statistics I learned that more than 39 million worldwide have been infected. We don't know how Carlos got the disease, because at this point no one knew much about him.

Back to my resource, I spoke with a nurse, "There is no cure for HIV, but you can control it with HIV treatment. Most people can get the virus under control within six months." And I asked the nurse what is, the difference between HIV and AIDS, and she explained, "is that HIV is a virus that weakens your immune system. AIDS is a condition that can happen as a result of an HIV infection when your immune system is severely weakened." I get to know also the three stages of HIV, and I was wondering which one possible Carlos had may have suffered from if he had it for sure. It was a conversation between them, could it be gossip? Carlos told me stuff but really don't know. The fact is no one in the cabin was infected.

35

Maybe, Carlos was in stage one, feeling well and decided to come with us. We didn't see any sign of sickness from him. Carlos was feeling well. But the sad truth is that many never know because Carlos seemed to be living an active life, and I learned that it's important to know that you can still spread HIV to others even if you feel well.

All the articles that I read about the HIV were helpful. It was a way to be educated and understand when you have intercourse with those around you someone may have had the virus and are careless even regarding a loved one. And the more I read articles and medical reports about the virus, I understood that people of all sexes and sexual orientations can get infected with and spread HIV but it is especially common in the gay and bi-sexual community.

After days, we got the results from Carlos. He

picked up the virus at the tattoo shop, by the owner using an infected needle. Months later we found out from a news broadcast that the store was closed because of the unsafe use of infected needles and exchange of needles, and we all knew that Carlos did a dragon tattoo at his arm, very pretty. When I saw it, "I told him, wow, that is one big dragon!"

And he said, "Yes, and I plan to do another one on my back."

I said, "You are brave, because I'd be so scared to do that," and later we learned that the owner disappeared.

I was fine considering the circumstance surrounding this episode, where I had to testify. This time I was very sad because Carlos was a good person, very classic and very educated. So I was brief, presenting my thoughts without wasting my words. I told everyone that we needed to get together to find safer places for people that wanted to get tattoos. Those places at the time did connect from the dangerous to old used needles. I knew we must get together to find justice for people like Carlos. Get the police involved, teach at school and let people know everything about HIV and giving them resources and a chance to live. Lack of resources is a wasted minute of your life. That was our goal: to show that people like Charles or Carlos should not die because of lack of information and carelessness. And be free to share if you got the virus. I believe that Carlos would know this, but since he was not feeling very sick, he assumed that he had a minor illness.

And watching him more and more around us, I would say that he was trying to be closer to Lucia. I was surprised when Ricardo told me he heard that Carlos got the HIV virus. At first sight I thought that he was a gay man. It was my reaction at the time. And I felt embarrassed to just assume my mental thoughts without knowing anything about the truth. That assumption is from a non-educated person; in contrast Lucia seemed more educated about the virus. A close friend of her family died with complications of the AIDS. Lucia said that "the family became so much closer to her family, that the parents baptized her at the age of two years. The family's son was already sixteen years old."

We had to learn a bit how to deal with the situation. "Zuze," she said, "the boy's name. he's been struggling with HIV and AIDS for about two years. As a family we tried to learn and give as much love as we could because my parents were not yet open regarding what to do. To Lucia, Carlos had been sick and not getting well for some days in the cabin. This was, for her, an eye-catching example that something was wrong.

No further investigation, no social person or "child services" at our door, at least this was what everyone was told.

Ricardo said, "No one has showed up at my door anymore, with one exception, the police wanted to know again why Carlos and Richard fought the day before Charles's death. I was expecting the police to interrogate me again." Ricard continued, "This happened because the officer who interrogated me forgot her file at the cabin and I took it. So, they didn't have my report. I didn't return the report because the officer was changing my words for his words. He said, "Every time I said something, he paraphrased it differently and I didn't like it." That was one of the reasons that I did not return his report."

I began my experiments at the Lab with materials that had been sent from China and European; then I became responsible to get the report and verify each box. With the help of Mariana and Paulo, we got the position at the company. I took the test first, I passed, and the company called me for an interview. I had never before had a test from a company and then the interview. The last time I did tests and exams was in order to attend college.

In fact, at the company, I did a lab test, wrote

an exam, and sat for an interview that was more complicated and intense. I had a habit of not following instructions very well, and I did not get the results accurate. I was growing up without being given the time and the patience to get things right. All too often I let myself become irritated, and then my project destroyed itself. I again heard my mother saying, "You are exactly like your grandfather, he enjoyed doing things and building, but without tolerance—without steadiness he gave up and he became a lab assistant. Not excited to be an assistant, he took another position at the company. However, he never forgot the fact that he would be a good engineer if he didn't let the impatience control him." Of course, again, bring in the family cycle, but I put myself on a course to guide me to focus and follow directions.

Then I had an opportunity, and I found some ways to not let me get trapped into the family cycle. I don't know about you, but it seems that everything that is bad or that does not work, they say Oh! That's normal, it should happen, and it already happened in the family. I gave my mother a very bad look and I said to her, "I am not like your father. I have constantly been accused of that. I must admit that I've had to get my butt kicked and each kick sent me a new message--that I must see myself as a completely new person, and this new person that is me, sometimes scares me a little.

During the course my patience was measured. I did the course for six months. It was very helpful, and I wish that I could practice yoga, because one day I put myself on the yoga program and quickly it changed my moods. Always have God as your guide. I'm not alone anymore. I practice yoga regularly and I invite God to be with me all the time.

I told my mother, "I'll not be like anyone else." I laughed. " "To be me is enough to keep me busy'." Constantly, I have to find myself and remain familiar with me. To find me sometimes I have to be with my friends and family, that is true, because they've brought out a little or a lot from inside me. To be honest, I wanted to test who an easy-going person is because by now I had not been fully tested.

I knew with my Lab project I needed to focus and give no chance for mistakes and no room for error. I expected the project to be done on time and with success. The company vision was in the hand of the intellectuals from Japan, and I should not let it down. Inside of each tube the portion had to be exactly shaped like my hope, and I said, "Our project will be in the hands of the managers tomorrow and presented the following morning to the Japanese representatives.

Paulo said, "Like what we worked hard for and we did a good report."

And I said, "It was definitely a great report."

After all the hard work and without explanation the Japanese representatives did not approve our project. I took all my free time to develop this project. It was simple, but it worked.

I'm glad that they didn't like it because later the company exposed the project at a scientific showcase as plain with no expectation and was selected to continue with the project at least. I have had a chance to be part of a big event, this time no interrogation and no other kind of pf services, just a big check from the company that they later gave to us as extra. I hope this result shows that I broke the cycle in those days, that I was still hearing from family and my friends saying that the parents always compared me with someone else in the family, and the sad or the lucky part of my life, and I will probably not completely unclothe my family cycle in this lifetime, and I have a coincidental behavior that may follow me as a birthright. It will be completely my choice joined together with my family's values as a child. I have no choice; I can gain the ability to understand, and I've caught the fact that everything does not come

to us as a fairy-tale. And I would not be able to resolve all issues. And I remember, in my house, everything was resolved with excuses, that "we as parents
understand because we were born to be this way,
and things will pass and everything will be normal
again..."

My parents' statements and the way they
viewed the world in some ways brought me to
conform when I think that these convictions result
eventually in a destiny that goes and returns like an
ocean tide. I called it a purpose, a chance, and I do
not look back. I'm looking straight into the direction
that I want to be. It took me a whole of trainings and
many dreams and I keep walking through my imagi-
nations, that I look over my past, and I can see one
thing my own face. I tried walling through the night
with a high expectation of a softy, and a natural way
extending my capacity to processing, my first family's stonewashed path.

In a different place I see my family and friends
from my schooltime, and I see my father and my
mother's ancestor's familiar behavior I felt uncomfortable carrying too many traditions and attitudes,
and behaviors that I didn't like, but I assume those
behaviors because they are there. It seems a simple

thing, like two being born together somewhat a physical part of your body—a finger, a leg, eyes... And some attitudes are equal to your father's or your mother's. I didn't want to follow, but when I see I already did exactly the same. And usually at first I said to my mother, "That is crazy."

My younger brother, he likes to cook, but it has to be exactly the way my grandmother usually cooks. So, to tell how, his preparation and cooking seems to take forever, and he uses all the spoons around him to test the food every time. That seemed fun, but I hated it because I was the one to clean up after him. The sink was a disaster. I said to my mother one day, "I will not clean the dishes; it is much too messy,"

And she said, "You didn't have a chance to see how your grandmother magically cooked and baked. You never took the time and great effort to learn grandmother's cooking, so it was okay that it is running in the family."

And I wrongfully thought the cycle can't be changed, it can only be re-shaped. But there are so many things every day from my family lore to gradually shape the family in the present or sometimes guide us to outline the best and ignore the ghosts and dark sides trailing far behind in the family tradition.

WAKE ME UP BEFORE SUNLIGHT

How is Lara today? Lara is saying, "I know that my life is the project of dreams; it is the aspiration for reality. And, I thought, all things come to my life because I'm given the opportunity for these good or bad things to be part of my life," As with many literary works, the seeking was a result of my own state of mind.

When I idealized, and I started to understand my state of living, I sought the help of the expressive past and present moments of my life, and the facts that surround me such as nature, love, the moon, and the silence ... all these things bring me a veritable basket of questions. And the stranger thought it was through my silence that I learned that I was supposed to be honest. And, I felt relieved with no reason to be unhappy—only to be natural.

Walking into my greater intimacy at the time,

silence provided me some moments for a great start. I learned from my great-grandfather how their lives were a continuous process of creation, and with a great sensibility of achievements that contributed to the development of a new generation. All the experiences acquired with these achievements brought my grandfather a sense of a different world with a comprehensive vision, a vision of peace.

For many years I had seen the impossible become possible. I had been seeking a permanent recovery from my past. Others see and wait for something to arrive with hope enough to move the world, so they can catch their belongings. Some will speak from their inner voice as peace in the midst of personal chaos, others will claim universal peace.

There is a time for everything in life, and now we need to face the group and say goodbye. But before we say goodbye for a while we set up a weekend trip to a closer beach. And we just started to talk about family lore, since everyone knows we're married and with children.

And I said, "When you have a group of friends, it seems we also have different experiences, a new vision, which friend you will follow, which ones you do not want to follow, how you decide to treat your enemies. And who will follow you? As a family tradition, it brings up the same idea of who you will follow, or who will follow you afterward.

"Mariana," she said, "it would be easier to not follow tradition too much and not too long, because we may miss the opportunity to discover new things. She said that she and Paulo stayed for about two years in Australia. After two months, Paulo already was missing his culture and the way his mother cooked and everything else, on the other side. Mariana also said, tradition is the past basic. She needed to pass to her kids a new experience. Lucia seemed to have a different idea about family tradition. And I asked her, "Lucia, it seems that you didn't follow either of your parents."

And she said, "No, not my parents, but my great-grandmother. My mother was always saying, that I got the best of the family, be patient, no matter what the situation is, and at the same time, when my father heard my mother saying that, he jumped into the conversation and said so passively and patient that I forgot to respond and to do things on time. I am so relaxed, then comes the negative side of my heritage.

Paulo and Francisco arrived later, after they finished their work. Fridays going to the beach always meant a big traffic jam. And Paulo said to Francsico, "Let's leave before the busy hours and do this short-cut my father just told me about."

CONCLUSION

It is simple knowledge, but when it comes to minor or major decisions, I say, "We always go to the wisdom that brings us closer to our family lore. No matter what circumstances are necessary to solve the problem, we find the answer in our traditional experiences.

Today I see my life as a landscape, an image lived or dreamed, the melodramatic moments that are impossible to avoid when that feeling comes from love or antipathy from relatives. I smiled and said, "Family always will be valued after tears, after drama, but it will define a consciousness full of awareness and choices."

When I started writing this book, it was based on a short story "Blood Moon." I felt something profound as I developed the story, realizing that humanity was looking for a cycle of conflict linked to anguish and imbalance of achievements. But I tried through simplicity and sensibility to give it a satisfying ending in Bloody Moon, as well as in signpost risks--facts that marked my life. In the manner in which the fictional aspects, like dreams, were written into my life, thus I am satisfied by quenching the thirst of those dreams; I have been worried about a single place: my silence, my inner circle of God, close family, and dear friends where I felt safe...

But when I sought after my heritage, I felt I had achieved my goal. I believe I've been able to focus much closer and also more profoundly. I rested on the awareness that exists within the human legacy. I'm smiling in the hope that someday I'll allow myself to look up in search of more things that are familiar to me.

ACKNOWLEDGMENTS

Growing up, I heard so many stories from my family and friends, and often it was hard to decipher if they were true, but I couldn't let these stories fade away.

Thank you to my family, my husband, my goddaughters, and my friends for sharing their stories, in any way they could. Through their stories, I was able to put this novel together.

I would also like to give a special thanks to everyone who have taken the time to grab and read one of my books. Finally, I would like to thank God for all his blessings, and I am very grateful for every single thing with which I have been blessed.

Thank you to all for your love and support. Thanks to the team at the Outskirt Press for shaping this story into a novel of interest.